The Promise of Moonstone

The
PROMISE of
MOONSTONE

A Novel

Pat Engebrecht

BEAUFORT BOOKS, INC.
New York / Toronto

Library of Congress Cataloging in Publication Data

Engebrecht, P. A.
The promise of moonstone.

Summary: A young ballet dancer faces a crucial
turning point when her teacher-mother is injured.
[1. Ballet dancing—Fiction. 2. Mothers and
daughters—Fiction]   I. Title.
PZ7.E6986Pr   1983   [Fic]   82-20659
ISBN 0-8253-0123-8

Published in the United States by Beaufort Books, Inc.,
New York. Published simultaneously in Canada by
General Publishing Co. Limited

Printed in the U.S.A.   First Edition
10 9 8 7 6 5 4 3 2 1

Designer: Ellen LoGiudice

To every mother
and daughter who has
misunderstood

The milky glow of the moonstone
Waxes and wanes with the moon.
The pearl of June,
Once in a blue moon,
Lights the way through the
Dark, dank tomb
Bringing the spirit safely home.

1

"Annya, aren't you ready yet?" Her pet name for her mother sounded sharp even to Kristina's ear. Practice hadn't started and already she was taut with agitation. Maybe it would be different this time. Maybe her mother wouldn't be so critical. She didn't think she could take even one word, not after all Mr. Fellini's bullying.

She put the needle on the record. Why couldn't her mother be on time? She knew they practiced at three. Strains of the Tchaikovsky waltz soothed her as she gathered her long auburn hair, twisting it into a thick, loose cord, and then flipped it on top of her head fastening it securely. Methodically, Kristina slid her feet into the scuffed, almost tattered, ballet slippers and laced them tightly, rising to her toes several times testing them for comfort. Unlacing the left shoe, she frowned, smoothed the ribbon, then laced it again. Satisfied at last, she moved to the long mirrored wall, placed her hand on the bar worn smooth from her touch, and began her preliminary exercises.

Caught up in the music, she stretched slowly and rhythmically, loosening each muscle with the care and knowledge of an experienced dancer. After a few minutes she called again, "Annya?"

The door opened and her mother hurried into the room running her fingers through her tight russet curls.

"Why are you always late?" The criticism in Kristina's voice was thinly veiled.

"Look, I'm sorry." She tugged at her dark green leotard. "You can start without me, you know." The scattering of freckles across her nose was more evident now that her summer tan had begun to fade.

She moved in beside Kristina and the two of them began to work in unison bending, stretching. This was the comfortable part of the practice: the time Kristina looked forward to. The silent sharing of an art they both loved. For the past ten years she and her mother had worked out at the practice bar escaping into a magical world of princes and swans, of dolls and soldiers. Although outsiders considered it make believe, for Kristina it was the real world—the world where she planned to spend her life. Not an easy existence but one filled with sweat and effort, thrills and disappointments, and mostly filled with discipline.

Their coloring was the only physical trait Kristina and her mother shared. Kristina's slight, boyish figure belied her sixteen years. She would always be small and wispish; where her mother was round, her muscles firm, her bosom high and full. The mirror played tricks with its imagery, etching a soft childishness about the mother with her short, curly bob; while the daughter's reflection was edged with a tinseled, bony strength. Controlled. Unyielding.

They moved from simple stretching to a drill routine that included all the fundamental moves of the ballet: the jetés, arabesques, pas des chats, and the most difficult fouettés. It was in the drill that one became aware of the difference between mother and daughter. It was evident even to a layman. Where Kristina worked at perfecting each individual movement, her mother moved loosely sliding from one to the other, a lanquid approach far less disciplined. That was where the trouble always began.

After they had worked together on the drills, they took turns doing short routines from individual ballets. Anna first. She flew loosely through a series of jetés, arabesques. Her leaps were high and lovely. There was something unique about her undisciplined dance that created excitement. There was a subtlety in her head, her hands... her every move. To the critical eye her moves were imperfect, sometimes even sloppy, but she had a flair. Her interpretation was spontaneous and imaginative. Spinning to a stop at the bar, she leaned against the wall and watched Kristina who tightened beneath her scrutiny. She could feel her mother's criticism, echoing in the recesses of the room, even before she started. Closing her ears to it, listening only to the music, she began. Her movements were clean and precise each blending perfectly into the other. Although technically far superior to Anna's, the excitement was missing from Kristina's routine. Anna knit her brow concentrating on her daughter's dancing.

"No. No. No! Not so rigid. Your routine is too mechanical. Predictable. Where is your imagination?" Kristina stiffened at the impatience in her mother's voice. The old, familiar resentment began to rise, and she had to bite back the words that banged around inside her head. She had practiced them so often that they were as familiar as an old tune, yet she had never uttered them aloud.

"No. You're bending your knees all wrong. Like this."

Kristina stopped, heels flat, watching but not seeing; listening but not hearing. She would tune her mother out; Kristina's dancing would never please her. There was no convincing Anna that there was a different way from hers. Kristina had given up trying. When she told Mr. Fellini, her dance coach, about her mother's criticism, he had assured her that interpretation would come, that first she must work on technique and precision. *"Discipline... Your mother lacks discipline!"* Fellini's words echoed as she watched her mother demonstrating. She finished with a flourish and turned to Kristina.

"Now, you try it."

Kristina did not move.

"Come on. It's easy."

Something inside her, something that had been building for a long time, snapped. "No!" She stood defiantly.

Her mother's mouth dropped in surprise.

"No! No! No!" The words came pouring out. "What makes you such an authority? You would think you had been a prima ballerina. What was the total of your career? Three bit parts in the New York Ballet, then you copped out for marriage. Well, I'm different. I've got what you didn't . . . discipline and dedication. Who asked you anyway?" Kristina's feet were spread wide apart, her hands on her hips. Her heart was thundering in her chest.

Her mother's voice was calm. "No, you didn't ask me, but I can . . ."

"I know." Kristina held up a stiffened hand as if warding off physical blows. "You can tell me what I'm doing wrong, and you do—over and over and over—like a broken record."

"Look, Kristina . . ." Exasperation had begun to creep in Anna's voice. "You say you want to be a ballerina. Well, it's tough. You . . ."

"You don't think I'm good enough." Kristina grew more rigid in her defiance.

"I didn't say that."

"But you don't, do you?" Her question was sharp, demanding an answer.

"Do you know how few ballerina's really make it? Even I . . ." Anna stopped, threw up her hands in a helpless gesture.

There. She'd almost said it. Kristina sucked in her breath.

"Even you didn't make it, and you're so much better than I am!"

"I didn't say that."

"No, but that's what you meant."

"Kristy . . ."

Her words were like the mercury from a broken thermometer, once freed they took on life and thrust of their own. Kristina could not gather them back.

"Why do you always butt into my practices anyway? I'm better off without you! I don't need or want you!" Her words echoed loudly. Instantly, Kristina was sorry. Her mother turned away from her, but not before she had seen how much her words had hurt.

Anna left her standing at the bar. The door clicked shut quietly. No anger, no recrimination.

"I've got discipline . . ." Kristina searched for the defiance and anger that had pushed her, but there was only an empty feeling. The record stopped. The silence was punctuated by the echoing of her own raspy breathing. Her solitary figure, shoulders drooping, reflected from the mirrored wall.

Oh hell! She was right; she could practice alone. Kristina sucked in her breath and walked over to reset the needle. She returned to the bar, raised her arm over her head, placed her feet into perfect position, and went up on her toes where she stood poised like a young wood nymph. Suddenly, she dropped flat on her heels. Of course she didn't mean it. Ballet without Anna? Unthinkable. If only she could make her mother understand. Ballet was the battleground that lay between them. They both loved it; they both were good dancers. Kristina didn't understand the conflict. Kristina was good . . . no matter what Anna said. She was different from her mother, but in her own way she was very good.

Giving in to her misery, Kristina threw herself across the

bed. She needed Annya. . . . She rolled the pet name for her mother across her tongue with pleasure. "You call your mother by her first name?" one of the girls at school had asked.

She didn't understand. No one did, not even her father. Annya was more than her mother: she was friend, adviser, confidante. There was no part of her life that didn't revolve around Annya. She remembered back when she was fourteen.

"Why don't boys like me, Annya?"

"What makes you think they don't?"

"Nobody asked me to the dance. Almost everyone else is going. Even Ellen."

"Who's Ellen?"

"Ellen Flatner. She's fat with buck teeth and . . . "

"Who's she going with?"

"Bruce Poesy."

"Is he nice?"

"You kidding? He's awful. He's got zits all over and is always leering at you and . . . "

"You wouldn't want to go with him?"

"Not in a hundred years! I wouldn't be caught dead with him."

"Who else is going?"

"Well, there's Mary Jane. She's going with Joey. He's six inches shorter than she is. And Betsy, she's going with Tom. He's the mathematical genius. Wears glasses this thick and all he does is grunt when you try to talk with him."

"Who would you like to go with?"

"Well . . . " She thought for a minute. "I guess there's not anyone but maybe Jeff. He's tall and blond. Runs the mile in track and does the pole vault and . . . "

"Who's he going with?"

"I don't think he's going."

Anna chuckled. "I think you have the question all wrong."

"What do you mean?"

"Instead of why don't the boys like Kristina? I think it's why doesn't Kristina like the boys?"

She started to protest then stopped and smiled. "You're right. Most of them are so dumb. They spit on the sidewalk, tell awful jokes, and are always ogling Janice's big boobs." She sighed looking at herself. "Not all of us are so fulfilled. Not that I'd want to be built like that. . . ."

"What great ballerina ever was?"

She looked at her mother and started to giggle, "Well, you . . ."

"Ah hah, the very reason I never made it. The director took one look at me and yelled, 'You . . . with the big boobs . . . out!' "

Kristina sighed. That's the way it was with her and Annya. They could talk about anything. They were friends, confidantes. The joy she and Annya shared excluded much of the world. Their relationship filled Kristina's need so completely that she sought no outside friends . . . a sore point with her father. She chafed at his criticism that she and her mother spent too much time together, that she needed friends her own age. He was just jealous. What did she expect? He was always too busy to share his time with them. Even though he worked at home, Kristina saw less of her father than did most of her friends. It seemed that an architect's life was full of deadlines.

The sound of the record echoed. Kristina raised up, cupping her chin in her hands, and stared out over the ocean. Her thoughts, the argument jumbled about in her mind leaving confusion and sorrow. Unseeing, she watched the waves roll in. Distant specks of moving figures brought her mind into focus.

She'd never seen people so far out on the beach before—

far past the normal sandy limits. Curious, she crawled off her bed and stood before the great spans of glass. It was the lowest tide she'd ever seen.

A light rap sounded on the door. She turned just as it swung open.

"Well, don't just stand there. Imagine all those crabs out there just waiting for us to scoop them up."

Kristina searched her mother's face. Her eyes were clear, hazel-green. There was no accusation, no blame as she had expected. The heaviness inside her lifted escaping through a wide grin.

Anna was dressed in hacked-off jeans, sweat shirt, and ragged sneaks. There was that familiar surge of energy radiating from her that always made Kristina feel more alive when with her. Happiness swelled replacing the misery and guilt she had been feeling. Anna turned and started back into the hall.

"Wait!" Kristina called. "I'll get my shorts."

"I'll wait out on the deck. I've got to get the nets and rakes."

She really wasn't mad. Kristina could tell. She flew to her dresser and yanked open the drawer pawing through the clothes. Not finding what she wanted, she slammed it shut and opened the next. She'd tell her. First opportunity she got, she'd tell her mother she was sorry. She hadn't meant what she'd said. Of course she needed and wanted her. Ballet without Annya? That was as unthinkable as life without Annya.

2

"Come on, let's go." Kristina started headlong down the path, her long hair flying loosely as she leaped, sure footed, from one ridge to the next, oblivious of the speed of her descent. Anna picked her way lightly but more slowly.

It was a rare day for October. The sun was warm and the sky that dark cobalt blue that can look unreal on a canvas. The gulls shimmered silver and white against its depth. They circled and cried out welcoming Anna and Kristina.

"Come on, Annya. Don't be so old and slow!" Kristina darted in and out among the outcropping of rocks. Finally, Anna rose to her challenge and chased her daughter through the shallow rivulets left by the receding tide out to the rocky hunch of Whalebone Ridge.

They paused at the first large pool. The water was so clear that it magnified the beauty of the pale-green and pink sea anemones that lay in full bloom waiting for the careless meandering of small bits of sea life. Tiny hermit crabs scurried about the bottom along with a school of darting finger-length fish that had been trapped by the receding tide. Dark-black mussels, almost obscure in the shadows, grew thickly on the jagged rocks.

The two of them remained motionless as they squatted low watching the drama before them. Finally, Kristina leaned over and reached into the pool. She pried loose a large mussel. First she placed the tip of the shell into the largest anemone that closed immediately trying to engulf the intrusion in its midst. Kristina held it for a moment then threw it high into the air amidst the flock of circling gulls. There was a loud screech. A large gull dived catching the shell mid-air, swooped off to a pile of rocks, circled for a moment making sure he was alone, and then dropped the mussel on the rocks cracking it. He dived immediately to collect his dinner.

The flock of gulls hovering over Kristina and Anna grew more restless and raucous in their cries. Kristina threw several more mussels into their circling midst before turning back to her mother. "Come on. Let's go out to the point. I've never been out that far before."

The two of them picked their way through the wet, slimy ridges being careful not to lose their balance. "Look at that!" Kristina stood looking down into a huge tidal pool teeming with some of the largest crabs she had ever seen. "Are we going to feast tonight!" She grabbed her net and set about chasing the scurrying crustaceans. The buckets would be easy to fill but heavy to carry. Kristina lost all sense of time in her efforts to catch the crabs. "Look at that one, Annya, and that!" She dipped for crab after crab.

Neither of them was aware of the change, of the disappearance of the gulls, of the ominous silence that settled over Whalebone Ridge. Finally, Kristina sensed something. She straightened, leaned on the handle of her net, and looked skyward.

"I wonder what happened to the gulls?"

Anna paused. She too looked skyward and then turned toward the sea. The two of them stood, silhouetted against the blue. Kristina stared at the oncoming wave. A low rumbling overcame the silence. "Oh my God!" She was jerked back to reality by her mother's words, "Run! Run, Kristy, run!"

They dropped their crabbing tools and started clambering over the rocks slipping and sliding on the wet algae. Kristina was well ahead of her mother when she heard Anna cry as she stumbled. She stopped and turned, but her mother was up and running again. "Keep going, Kristy, I'm all right. I'm coming," she called.

The rumbling turned to a roar that filled her head and mind. She dared not look back but leaped from stone to stone calling, "Annya?"

"Keep going!" Her mother's voice could barely be heard above the roar and then a high-pitched scream stopped Kristina. She turned. Anna had been caught up as if by a giant hand and hung suspended high above; she too was being sucked up and up, her head filling with the fury. She gagged and gasped feeling herself tumbling over and over into the thrashing black water all the time struggling for light and air.

As suddenly as the thrust upwards began it ceased, and Kristina was held suspended for a moment and then was falling—down, down toward the jagged rocks below. Just before she was dashed against them, the water rushed in beneath her, catching her, tossing her upward into the wave that crashed upon her pressing her down like nothing she had ever known. Her lungs were bursting in her struggles and she sensed the blackness spreading within her.

Unconsciousness had almost engulfed her when she felt herself pressed against an outcropping of rock. She clutched at it struggling to find something to cling to, a crevice to wedge her fingers or toes. She searched frantically before finding a small niche. Her legs and feet, long since shorn of sneakers, instinctively sought something to wrap around. The water dropped away, but returned again and again relentlessly tearing at her trying to dislodge her. She clung fast to her ledge.

And then the wave was gone. Almost as suddenly as it had

rushed in on them, it returned to sea leaving Kristina gasping for breath clinging tightly to her rocky perch. She threw her head back trying to clear her eyes of the stinging, salty, sand-filled water.

"Annya?" Her voice was small and weak. "Mother!" Fear pushed the word to a high wail. Frantically she searched the heaving sea until she saw her mother still being tossed about in the water that washed over the ridge.

"Annya!" Forgetting her fear, she loosened her grasp and let herself half-slide, half-fall down her rocky precipice ignoring the sharp jabbing pain of the rocks gouging at her legs and thighs. She had only one thought, one goal. Slipping and falling over one crusty rock after another, she made her way to the ridge where she had last seen her mother.

Kristina searched the waves straining her eyes against the brilliant reflection of the sun on the water. The fear returned, catching up in her throat, thickening her tongue, so that she could not swallow. Annya was gone. Disappeared. "Annya! Annya!" She heard a moan and turned. Relief buckled her knees and she almost fell. Her mother had been thrown into one of the inner pools. An incoming wave rushed in picking her limp form up lightly. Kristina lunged forward grabbing her before she could be washed out to sea.

3

Kristina sat in the dark, plush office with her father. The doctor was talking on the telephone. He did not look at them immediately after hanging up but straightened the already neat piles of papers on his desk. He cleared his throat several times. Kristina squirmed at his avoidance. Obviously, he was searching for the proper words.

"Well, Mr. Lowrey, Kristina..." he hesitated. "I guess you know we've done all we can." He stopped his fussing, looked at her father, and then over to her. "She'll be better off at home. It will be hard at first, but...I..." He opened his suit coat and reached into the inside pocket. "I know a woman. Martha. Martha McGuire." He pushed a card across the desk to Rodney Lowrey. "She's a gem. You might even get her to live in."

"What do you mean you've done all you can?" Kristina had moved to the edge of her chair. She tried to control the pitch of her voice, tried to swallow her fear. "Are you telling me that my mother will never get any better. That..."

"Oh, she'll get stronger once she gets used to... well, there will be a period of time before she'll be able to accept..."

"Accept what?" Kristina interrupted.

"The fact that she's crippled."

"No!" Kristina jumped up. She clasped her hands over her ears. "No! Annya will dance and run again. You just wait. You don't know her. She will not be crippled!" She stood quivering, staring defiantly at the doctor, then she turned and fled from the pity in his face; but she could not escape the echoing of his words.

Kristina stood in the doorway watching her father struggle to move his large drafting desk. "Give me a hand, would you, Kristina?"

"What are you doing?"

"Anna is going to need a room of her own. I thought this would be the best."

"But this is your office."

"I know, but it has the nicest view."

"But . . . well . . . it seems kinda silly to move all your things. I mean Annya will be up and around in no time."

Studying her thoughtfully, he started to say something and then changed his mind. "Well, I think I'll go ahead. Make yourself useful and grab an end."

Kristina shrugged. "I still think it's silly, but . . ." She took a firm hold of one end of the desk and lifted.

They worked in silence moving the furniture, books, and supplies. When they were through, she returned to the gutted room pausing at the door. The emptiness of it slapped at her like a premonition leaving a hollow, scary feeling deep inside her. She closed her eyes, shuddered, and turned away bumping into her father. He reached out to steady her.

"I'm sorry." She looked up into his eyes and for the barest moment she knew that he felt it too . . . the same foreboding. This sharing startled her. It had never happened before. They were strangers. Her life had been filled with her mother and dancing. His with his wife and his work. Kristina had learned very early in life that even though daddy worked at home there was not time for her—for architects were continually faced with deadlines. "Do not disturb" she had been warned. If deadlines measured greatness, Rodney Lowrey was indeed a great architect.

It was her father who broke the silence. "Well, let's get on with it."

"What can I do?" It was the question she had been asking herself over and over ever since the accident.

"You know those old ballet posters Anna collected? Go get them."

And so it started, the creation of Anna's miniature world. He mounted a track along the south wall and hung her favorite plants: the prolific spider plant heavily endowed with babies, the green and pink geranium begonia, the rampant creeping Charlie. He matted some delicate water colors of familiar wild flowers and hung them. The two of them made the ballet posters into a floor to ceiling collage. They brought all of Anna's gardening books into the room along with her tapes of Tchaikovsky, Chopin, and Rimski-Korsakov.

It was three days before the room was finished to their satisfaction. Kristina stepped back surveying their handiwork. It was perfect except for one thing: the ugly steel hospital bed that dominated one corner.

They brought her home. Not the same Anna who had gone crabbing with Kristina on Whalebone Ridge. That woman who had been filled with an eagerness for life, who was warm, loving, and reassuring, had been lost in the turbulence that day leaving a quiet, remote, cold person Kristina did not know or understand. One she could not reach. God was it only two months—Kristina turned time over in her mind examining it like a coin. It was a lifetime and yet, she closed her eyes. It seemed only a moment ago that she and her mother had been together dancing at the bar. Try as she would, she could not shake the thought. She tried to shut her ears to her own voice, but the words hammered insistently within her.

"Why do you always butt into my practices? I don't need or want you!" It was her fault. Everything was Kristina's fault. If only . . . she would make it up to Annya. She would dedicate herself. With patience and discipline, she would see to it that Annya would defy them all. She *would* walk again. She would run through the surf and leap into those graceful fouettés that Kristina secretly envied.

Kristina picked her way over and around the piles of lumber and building material to where her father stood. "I don't see why you're going to all this trouble building a room and everything. We don't need anyone to take care of Annya. I will do it. She's my mother!"

He looked up from the sketches he had been studying. The worker's pounding continued. Kristina's heart was beating rapidly and her breath caught. It was silly to feel so nervous, after all he was her father. But there was no ease between them. No familiar paths. Her words erupted far more harshly than she had intended.

"I know, Kristina. But it's too much to expect. She needs constant care, especially at first. You have school and ballet. . . ."

"I'll quit ballet."

"Don't be silly. She wouldn't want that."

"Look, she's my mother and this is my . . ." She almost said fault but hesitated . . . "my responsibility. I don't want any stranger taking care of her."

"That's very noble, Kristina." He reached out and touched her. She shrugged his hand off jerkily. The way he said "noble" . . . it was almost like he was making fun of her. The tightness began to spread.

"I've met her, Kristina. She's a nice woman. Anna will like her."

24

"Well, I won't!" She whirled, almost tripping over a pile of two-by-fours. "I won't like her at all!" she shouted as she ran zigzag through the debris, away from her father. Down the beach path to the sea.

Every day Kristina rushed home from school. She had three weeks before Martha McGuire was scheduled to arrive. That would be enough. She would have Anna walking before then. She did not go to her room to practice but instead went straight to her mother's room.

"Hi, Annya, how was your day?" Her voice was high, filled with cheerfulness. It was always the same. Her mother sitting in her wheelchair staring out over the sea. She would turn slowly and look at Kristina as if she were a stranger.

"Fine. Just fine." Her words were polite, emotionless, empty. Then she would turn back to the window to resume her vigilance. It was as if she was searching for something.

Kristina swallowed trying to still the heaviness that churned inside her. As the days passed a quiet desperation began to grow. Her smile became wide and forced, her voice high with false gaiety, her routine set. She greeted her mother, threw her books on the table, and grabbed the hairbrush. She moved behind her mother and began to brush. There she was safe from her mother's eyes, which had become so distant. She brushed rhythmically chattering nervously about school nonsense. Finally, she would lay the brush aside.

"Time for your exercises, Annya." She moved around in front of her mother ducking her head as she knelt. She removed her slippers and began massaging her cold, clammy flesh, which soon turned rosy beneath the touch. Kristina chattered on as she worked. "That doctor . . . he's crazy! Not walk? Of course you'll walk and dance. He just doesn't know you like I do." She prattled on and on ignoring Anna's silence. "All we need to do is get a little blood down into the toes and start exercising them." She manipulated her mother's toes. "Okay, Annya, now all you have to do is move the big toe. Just the big toe." She'd pause watching, waiting. When nothing happened, she'd move to the next foot and start all over again trying not to flinch as she touched her mother's lifeless flesh. She continued chattering, ignoring the lack of response. Methodically, she raised and lowered each foot in the same precise, disciplined way she practiced her dancing. "All we need is time and patience, Annya. We'll show them." There was an urgency in Kristina's voice that echoed the desperation locked within her.

Time slipped by in a blur. The day Kristina had dreaded, quickly arrived. "Hello." Kristina held out her hand reluctantly to the short, earthy woman who smiled broadly.

"And you must be Kristina." The woman ignored the girl's hesitancy, clasping her hand warmly with both her own enthusiastically. "'Tis obvious you are Anna's daughter. A little more flesh on those bones and a real beauty you'll be blooming into."

Martha McGuire. You could almost smell the Scottish heather and hear the bagpipes. Her voice was loud and penetrating. Her eyes, the deep blue of a September aster, seemed to hold laughter puddled in them.

After showing her around the main house they took Martha to her room behind the garage. She stood in the open doorway her eyes large with wonder. She set her suitcase down and moved hesitantly over to the Ben Franklin fireplace. Gently, she rubbed her hand across it, then she moved over to the wall where a refrigerator and a small oven had been installed. She turned to look at them. Still she said nothing. Kristina had the feeling that silence was not Martha McGuire's usual reaction. Finally she made a weak movement with her arm.

"Is this truly me own room? With fireplace and all?"

Kristina couldn't help but feel a warmth for the woman whose eyes were shiny with wonder. There was an awkward pause and then Kristina, her voice filled with enthusiasm, pushed at her father. "Show Mrs. McGuire the bathroom." She bounced across the room and opened the door with a flourish. "Your bathroom, Mrs. McGuire."

"Now don't you be Mrs. McGuiring me, missy. It's Martha." She peeked into the bath and clasped her hands. "Oh my, how fancy." She turned back to Kristina's father. "It's all so grand," she whispered.

"Well . . ." He cleared his throat. "It doesn't have an ocean view or anything, and we've installed an intercom so that we might be disturbing you in an emergency."

"You feel free to be calling me any time you need me!" Martha added brusquely.

Kristina should have been happy. After all, Anna liked Martha and in just three weeks she had come to realize how absurd her insistence that she could take care of Anna had been. In a way she was relieved but that made her feel even more guilty. There was absolutely no reason that Kristina would dislike ever cheerful, plump Martha except . . . she smoked. That's what Kristina decided she didn't like about her. She was a chain smoker. Since she had arrived, the entire house reeked of the stale, nauseous odor.

Resent Martha, herself? Ridiculous. How could she resent the woman when it was obvious that she adored Anna and spoiled Rodney Lowrey rotten. It seemed to Kristina that her mother opened up more around Martha than she did for Kristina. Once she even heard them laughing.

There was no shared laughter between Kristina and her mother. Each day was the same. Anna silently watchful. Kristina working feverishly manipulating, exercising her mother's feet and legs. In spite of all their efforts, Anna's legs began to grow thin. The muscles began to shrink. With each passing day the guilt and loneliness within Kristina grew. She worked longer and harder exercising, rubbing, as if by sheer will and determination she could make Anna's legs grow firm.

"We can do it, Annya. Come on now," she would coax. It happened unexpectedly. She had come into the room as usual her voice high, a sound even she had come to detest. She brushed Anna's hair trying not to notice how it had changed. How dull it had become. After a while she laid the brush aside and moved around in front of her mother.

"Okay, this time we'll do it. Just a tiny bit. Just a beginning." She rubbed the toes. "Go ahead, Annya. Move the big toe. You can do it." She was not aware of the impatience that had crept into her voice.

"Leave me alone! Why don't you just leave me alone?" The words came out strangled and harsh.

All the frustration boiled up from within Kristina. She jumped up. "You're not trying! Goddamn it, you just sit there not even trying. How can you go on staring out that window like a zombie? Get up! You could if you tried." She leaned over and grabbed her mother by the arms pulling her up from the chair. "You might as well be dead if you aren't going to try!" Her mother's limp body collapsed against her.

"Kristina! For god's sake!"

She hardly even felt the sting of her father's slap. Suddenly, she was being pushed aside and he was there taking Anna into his arms. Kristina stood in a trance staring, feeling the redness of his handprint deepening and spreading across her face.

"Get out of here!" he hissed cradling her mother against him. Her hand flew up to her mouth holding back the bile that surged into her throat. She whirled and ran from the room, out of the house into the gray winter-whipped day plunging heedlessly down the steep path to the ocean.

4

Kristina hadn't meant those words any more than she'd meant her outburst the day of the accident. Of course Anna knew she didn't mean them. She had to know. She would make it up to her. She'd dedicate her whole life, she'd give up ballet, she become her mother's legs.

The three of them sat together listening as the melancholic strains of Chopin echoed the last notes. The record slowed and stopped. Anna started to wheel herself over to change it. "I'll get that, Annya." Kristina jumped up and dashed over to the record. She flipped it over and reset the needle. The music swelled.

"Where is my slide rule?" Her father looked about the room.

"I saw it over by my garden books." Anna started to turn her chair toward the table.

"I'll get it." Kristina was bounding across the room.

"Kristina," her father's voice was sharp bringing her up with a start, "let your mother get it."

"That's okay." Anna had stopped. She turned her chair back to her window and resumed her vigilance of the sea.

Rodney Lowrey glared at Kristina. What had she done? God . . . couldn't she do anything right? She turned and fled.

Hope should not die so easily. Kristina was ashamed especially when she watched her father and Martha both working so hard burning bright with hope for Anna. Why didn't they look at her. Anybody could see what was happening. The youthful muscles in her legs continued to shrivel into thin, limp strings. The color of her skin turned to a yellow-white. Even her hair, in spite of Kristina's brushing, had dimmed to a dull, rusty brown. It was all so confusing. Kristina didn't understand why, but she could see that her mother ws dying right before her eyes.

Resentment began to grow. How could she do that to Kristina after all they had been to each other? How could she desert her now when Kristina needed her more than she ever had? Why wouldn't she try? All she had to do was try. Kristina was so sure that her mother could walk if she only tried. She closed her eyes and once again Anna was there playing in the surf, crabbing in the pools, dancing at the bar.

It hurt too much. Kristina began drawing herself in tighter and tighter protecting herself from the pain. She stopped going to her mother's room after school. Instead she spent more and more time at the bar drilling and drilling. Hour after hour her music echoed through the house. At least there she was not alone. It was the only place where her mother—where Annya was beside her. In her dark green leotards, her tight russet curls shining in the sunlight, she leaped and spun.

"You'll have to be home by three." Kristina's father poured honey from a small pitcher onto his muffin.

"I can't. This is Wednesday. I have ballet from three to five." Kristina pushed the cereal bowl away from her in distaste. "Yuck! Why does Martha insist on cooking the oatmeal until it looks like baby cereal? Doesn't she understand the term quick cooking?"

Her father ignored her complaint. "You'll have to skip

ballet. Martha needs the day off, and I have a meeting I have to go to."

Kristina stopped buttering her toast and looked at her father. She had been half asleep but was alert now. He would never understand about ballet. He never even tried. Her nostrils flared and her eyes narrowed. Sarcasm dripped from her words. "Father, we're doing *Coppélia*. I'm dancing the lead. I have to show for rehersal." Her words were slow, deliberate.

"Missing one rehersal won't kill the production. They can work around you." The finality in his voice increased her anger. She watched as he rose wiping his hands on his napkin.

"You don't seem to understand. I *have* to show for rehersal."

"And just what do you propose we do, leave Anna here by herself?" His eyes had narrowed, his voice hardened. "Is dancing more important to you than your mother?"

Anger, hurt, indignation . . . it all churned inside Kristina. How dare he imply that she did not love her mother, that . . . she threw down the knife she had been holding and rose shakily. He stood across from her. "You never liked ballet anyway!" She could not stop herself. The words erupted, spilling forth. Words that had been hidden away. At first her voice was low and controlled, then rose rapidly.

"What right do you have to say a thing like that to me? I love Annya more than you ever thought of. What do you know? You are always too busy. You with your 'Do not disturb' sign. You've never had time for me. Always working. A deadline for this. A deadline for that. Always criticizing, telling Annya she shouldn't be with me so much."

Once Kristina had started there was no stopping. She was almost screaming. "I heard you telling her it was unhealthy the way we were. You were just jealous. Jealous because she

31

and I were so close. We didn't need you." Kristina hung on to the table for support. "Now . . . well it seems like you love her more now and have time for her now when you didn't . . ." Her heart was thumping heavily, her breath coming in short little gasps. The two of them stood face-to-face no more than an arm's length apart and yet separated by years of unspoken words. Kristina's accusation hung unfinished. Silence echoed stretching between them.

He studied her for a long moment and then he answered, his words soft and low. "She needs more love and attention now, Kristina."

The chiming of the entry clock nudged them back into their routine. He turned and removed his coat from the back of the chair. "I'm sorry. First things first. It just can't be helped."

He didn't go out the front, but turned and made his way back to Anna's room. He was never so hurried that he didn't take the time to share his plans for the day. Especially now that he was out of his office more often.

Kristina slumped into her chair and stared down the empty hall where he had disappeared. Her stomach was knotted in . . . was it anger? At what? After all it had been a simple request. What did she expect?

The soft sound of his voice echoed. Her resentment wilted. How did he do it? How did he look at that shrunken thing her mother was becoming with such concern and tenderness and yet never patronizing? He talked with her just the same as he always had, as if nothing had happened.

She closed her eyes and listened to the quiet sounds of his voice, saw him perched on the stool next to Anna his sketches unrolled. "Having a little trouble with J. B.'s house. It's the site we're worried about. He wants it here on the northwest corner, but I'm concerned about the pressure of the hill against the basement walls. I suggested he move it over to here, but then we have a landscaping problem. I told him I'd check with you and we'd come up with something. Think about it, would you? I'll be a bit late tonight. Got a meeting with the town board over that variance on Langely's property. You have a good day now, Anna." In her mind Kristina could see him kissing her, loving her, pulling her sweater close about her shoulders. She shuddered, feeling again that cold clamminess of her mother's skin.

How could it ever be the same? Would the Anna she knew and loved ever come back to them? If her mother wanted it bad enough. If she would only . . . "Your mother lacks discipline," Mr. Fellini's voice echoed. Kristina needed her so badly. Needed the love, the . . . there were no words to describe how her mother had made her feel. Was it all a dream? Was the warmth they had shared only in Kristina's heart? Had it really existed or was it a shadow of another life?

As she sat in English class, that morning's scene with her father floated in and out of Kristina's thoughts. One minute she was hot with indignation, the next she was cold with shame. She was so engrossed in her own thoughts that until the whispering of the two girls across the aisle caught her attention, she was unaware of the unusual activity at the front of the room.

"Jill Hangtree from Los Angeles." The teacher was introducing a new girl. Curiously, Kristina eyed her. She was tall and angular, and had chestnut hair that she wore twisted into a rather untidy knot leaving a halo of loose wispy hairs framing her high-cheeked, rather Indian-looking eyes. There was a strangeness about her. A presence Kristina decided that set the other girls on edge. She saw them eyeing Jill critically and whispering. Their reactions amused her. She felt apart from it all. She had always been apart, always watching; but it was only since her mother's accident that she had become aware of it.

"Doesn't she know miniskirts are out?"

"You'd think she'd take the time to comb her hair."

"My god . . . eye shadow!" Snatches of the female growling floated down the aisle and through the classroom.

Kristina watched Jill move from the front of the class down the aisle to the seat behind her. She had a peculiar walk. Smooth. Something rather ancient about it like a woman carrying a large jug on her head. She slid into the seat noiselessly. Kristina didn't turn but continued doodling on her notebook.

"Please copy the assignment on the board." Kristina felt a light tap on her shoulder. She turned.

Jill shrugged spreading her hands indicating her lack of pencil or paper. "You wouldn't happen to have a spare pencil, would you?"

They were wrong. Jill didn't wear eye shadow. Her lids were a natural pale translucent green. Her eyes, like pebbles in a stream bed, shadowed light and dark; but what Kristina noticed most was the fragrance surrounding her. What strange perfume had captured the odor of desert sage on a summer day?

"And a piece of paper? We got in so late last night, and our stuff hasn't arrived yet."

Kristina tore a page from her notebook and rummaged through her purse. "I'm sorry, it's not very sharp."

"That's okay. Thanks." Jill took the pencil and paper and started copying the assignment.

"Hey . . . your pencil." Jill's voice followed Kristina down the hall.

"That's all right." She paused, waiting. "You'll need it for your next class. By the way, my name is Kristina Lowrey. Hope you'll like it here. Where do you live?"

"On Shore Drive."

"Me too. What number?"

"I'm not sure. It's the old Miller place. Know it?"

"Sure. Everyone knows the old Miller place. It's supposed to be haunted you know."

"So we've heard." Jill didn't look concerned by Kristina's revelation. "A sea captain isn't it?"

"Yes. I think that's how the story goes. He always took his wife to sea with him despite his crew's insistence that it was bad luck. Well, it turned out bad luck all right. For her! No one knows for sure what happened, but one time she didn't come back. There was a big investigation. This was all years and years ago. He never went out after that. Just kind of boarded himself up in that house. They found him there. Had been dead for ages. It's sort of gross when you think about it. Heard any strange sounds?"

"No, but if he's still there, maybe I'll make friends with him and find out what really happened to his wife."

The easy way Jill said that made Kristina pause and really look at her. She was strange.

"Hey, Loony Tunes." Kristina stopped. Her whole body took on a wary edge. Jill looked at her curiously and then to the group of boys in the hall. There were three of them taunting a tall, thin boy.

"Do Bugs Bunny for us. Come on wiggle your ears. Hey, look at that you guys. He really can." They had surrounded the boy who was taller than any of them.

"Who's that?" Jill whispered.

"Paul Rolland." Kristina answered. "A friend of mine."

"How about your nose, can you wiggle your nose?" One of the shortest boys reached up and tried to pinch Paul's nose. Paul didn't strike out at him but launched into his wild stuttering, "Wh-a-a-t's u-u-p, D-Doc?"

"That's good. Didn't I tell you fellas?" They nodded their approval. "And how about the dance? Why don't you give us a demonstration? Is it like this?" The leader of the group rose up on his toes and started flapping his arms wildly.

Kristina shrank with embarrassment for Paul. Why didn't he . . . Jill left her standing there and walked up to the group. "You guys are real turkeys aren't you?"

The three of them stopped their wild imitations and turned on Jill eager to pounce. They paused, mouth open. Kristina was awed by the change she witnessed. All of their cockiness seemed to evaporate. They looked down and started to shuffle their feet. Finally one of them spoke.

"We were just having some fun with Loony Tunes. He don't mind." The speaker hesitated for a moment and then turned to his friends. "Come on, let's go." The three of them moved off down the hall.

Paul didn't look at Jill. He shoved his hands deep into his pockets and stared at the tip of his sneaker. Kristina came up to him and reached out touching his arm. "Paul?" He looked up. Relief swept across his face.

"Wh-a-a-t's u-u-p, D-Doc?"

"Paul," impatience crept into her voice, "this is Jill Hangtree. She's new." The boy turned to Jill.

"Ahhh." He was back to staring at his sneaker. "Hi." he muttered and then before Kristina could say anything he grinned a big wide grin. "Hey, do you know what one half the carrot said to the other?"

"Paul!"

"You're the tops!" Paul slapped his leg and started to laugh.

Kristina clenched her first. She'd like to knock some sense into him, but instead she said, "Would you tell Mr. Fellini I can't make it to practice tonight?"

All the foolishness dropped from his face. "But we're doing the kidnap scene. We can't do that without you."

"Well, you'll have to change it to something else because I have to go home early. Martha can't stay with Annya."

A look of genuine concern shadowed his face. His voice was soft. "How is your mother?"

Kristina actually looked at him for a moment. His hair was very black and curly against his fair skin. She was surprised to see the shadow of a mustache along his upper lip. His eyes, she'd always known, were blue, but where had those streaks of gray come from? She looked away strangely uncomfortable with his concern.

"Nothing's changed." She turned and moved down the hall toward her locker. Jill hesitated then caught up with her. They walked together in silence. As a rule Kristina would have found herself chattering nervously for she was uncomfortable in silence, but for some reason she didn't feel the need to talk. She felt a strange quietness in Jill's presence. Finally she said, "He's not that bad. Not really. I don't know what gets into him. I get so embarrassed and feel so sorry for him. Then I get mad. Why doesn't he punch those guys right in the mouth?" Again they walked on in silence. "He's a good dancer you know." Kristina went on. "He just might be great someday." Jill continued in her silence allowing Kristina her speculation. "He's so different when he dances. Strong, sure of himself."

The two girls paused at the locker. Jill watched as Kristina spun the combination, and then she reached out and touched her gently. They looked at each other. "I'm glad we moved here," Jill said softly. "I think it's going to be special."

Kristina felt a warmth rush through her. She'd never had a close friend before. "I'll see you tomorrow." Jill turned and disappeared down the hall.

5

Kristina swung down from the bus. "Night, George," she called flinging her jacket over her shoulder. She waited for the bus to pull away and then crossed the road to the mailbox. As she opened it, she heard the door bang and looked up to Martha's hurrying figure.

"Oh, there you be. Gotta catch my bus, missy. Your mother is fine. Should have some fresh air though on such a nice day."

She didn't pause in her headlong march down the path; her sensible, brown tie shoes slapping firmly against the warm brick. Her rust-plaid coat was buttoned snuggly in spite of the spring warmth. Her soft felt hat pulled securely over her tight curls that defied mussing.

Martha was a pillar of strength. Kristina was the first to admit it, but she couldn't help the way she felt. Martha had slipped into their household easing their adjustment to Anna's needs. Anna... what had become of Annya? Kristina didn't know why, but she could no longer bring herself to call her mother by that old pet name. It was one more loose piece that rattled around inside her head. She just couldn't call that stranger, that distant, cold, unloving... Kristina was shocked at the thought that had slipped into her consciousness. She shook her head pushing the thought back, back where she would not have to face it.

Although Martha had many habits that irritated Kristina, her warmth and concern for her mother were sincere and unlimited. She was always cheerful, clucking about Anna telling tales, gossiping, fussing, cleaning, assisting, going about doing the necessary things so matter-of-factly that nobody was embarrassed, even Anna.

At the sound of Martha's voice a funny feeling tightened and began to swell within Kristina. She tried to deny it, but it was there. Martha was good. Martha was kind. But Martha was Martha, and Kristina resented her very presence. It was an intrusion. Especially her protective, bossy attitude with Anna. Jealous? Kristina? Not a bit, but... well the house just wasn't the same and it was all Martha's fault. It didn't even smell the same, not with Martha's continuous smoking. That, Kristina decided again, was what she disliked about Martha.

6

Kristina watched the bus roll to a stop and the short, chunky woman clamber aboard. She sighed. There was no putting it off any longer. She picked up her books and headed up the path toward the house resolving with grim determination that it would be different this time. She would break through to Anna. She would start by telling her she didn't mean those words she had shouted about her not trying, about being better off dead. She was always saying things she didn't mean . . . like the day it had happened. Of course she wanted and needed Anna beside her. Ballet was not the same anymore. It would never be the same. How could it?

She knocked and pushed open Anna's door her wide smile carefully fixed. All her intentions were lost in the sound of her high, idiotic voice. "Hi, Anna, how about a walk?" If her mother noticed that Kristina no longer called her Annya, she made no indication except possibly to withdraw even more. If Kristina hadn't been so preoccupied with Anna's physical changes, she would have noticed her mother's more subtle reactions.

"It's really nice and warm today. I'll bet you're anxious to get out into that sunshine." Kristina didn't pause, but rushed on, "Where did Martha put your sweater? You know how cool the breeze can be." All her resolve vanished as she prattled on rummaging through a small chest. At last she found a black cardigan and pushed the drawer closed. "Here we go." She handed the sweater to her mother who ignored it.

"I don't want to go outside." Her voice was full of irritation.

"Of course you do. You love it outside. Come on, put on your sweater." Anna continued to ignore the sweater Kristina pushed at her. She glared at her daughter whose eyes skittered away. Kristina's voice became edged with exasperation. "Don't be difficult. You haven't seen your garden in over a week. Come on, put on your sweater."

Still Anna ignored the proffered sweater. Finally, Kristina shrugged, moved around behind her, and threw the sweater across her shoulders. Anna jerked as if she were trying to pull away from her daughter. Kristina swallowed at the hurt and anger that swelled within her, took hold of the chair, and started pushing it jerkily through the house.

They moved out into the garden onto the path that wound through the brilliant blooms of the low succulent ground cover. She took a deep breath and tried again. "Look at the ice plant, Anna. It really has grown hasn't it? Remember that first year?" Kristina remembered it all so clearly . . . as if it were yesterday. It was one of the few times she had seen her father get really angry with Anna and for once she had understood, had actually empathized with him. When Anna got involved with her garden, even Kristina felt left out. As critical as she was of her father, she had to admit that Rodney Lowrey was a very patient man. That day he'd come home tired and hungry and had found Anna on the hillside planting the hundreds of small ice plants. He stood watching for a time then finally asked, "What's for dinner?"

Anna straightened, rubbing the small of her back, "Oh, Rod, I'm sorry. I just haven't had time. Can you make yourself a sandwich? Careful . . . don't spill the fertilizer!"

41

He stumbled slightly as he backed into the pail of light green liquid.

"Why in the hell don't you let the workers plant this stuff? You don't need to be out here."

She paused, trowel in hand, her lips in a tight, thin line. "This is my garden and I intend to plant it not hire it out."

"Well, if you're so intent on doing the planting, maybe you could hire them to do the cooking!" He had turned and stalked off mumbling that he should be a goddamned plant; then she could feed him Rapid Gro.

Kristina waited for the loveliness of the garden to soothe her mother, to interest her. There must be something that would pull Anna from the shadowy retreat where Kristina could not reach her. How could she resist the beauty around her? Even Kristina found herself stopping to enjoy the fragile new shoots of the bearberry and the delicate snowflake blossoms of the spirea. She moved the chair slowly through the garden. If anything could spark a reaction in her mother, it would be her plants. She couldn't see the expression on her face, but from where Kristina stood, there was no sign that Anna was aware of the changes spring had inspired.

She commenced chattering again in that same false, bright tone she had acquired when attempting to communicate with her mother. "You're looking really great today, Anna. We'll get a little color in your cheeks, a little tan, and you'll be the same old knockout."

God why? She hated the inane sound of her voice prattling on in its lunacy. Why couldn't she just sit down and tell Anna how she felt. How much she missed her. How lonely her life had become. How sorry . . . for all her resolutions, she could not bring herself to apologize for those words. Couldn't bring herself to tell her mother how much she was hurting. What right did she have to complain? Time and again she had to stop herself from complaining about Mr. Fellini. She wanted to ask Anna's advice about the arabesque she couldn't quite perfect but bit back the words. She had done so many things wrong. How could she complain about an imperfect arabesque when Anna couldn't even walk.

If only she could hold her mother close and tell her of her need, but how could she? Kristina could now barely bring herself to touch Anna. She tried to hide the way she felt, but since that early hope had died, despair now filled her. Her mother would never walk. No way would Kristina want to live like that. There were moments when she understood Anna's retreat. She must hate her helplessness, her dependency, an existence so foreign to what she had been. What pleasure could life possibly hold for her. She would always be crippled! *I'd rather die*, she thought.

But Kristina discovered you did not just choose death. It was not as simple as that, any more than you chose life or your parents. It was not fair. Why Anna? Anna who had loved life and lived it with such enthusiasm. If... if... if. She shook her head to rid herself of her thoughts.

She continued pushing the wheelchair and its silent occupant through the garden and out along the hard-packed path high above the Pacific. Thin fingers of clouds had moved out across the sky stretching over the water like an open hand. Blue-green waves wrinkled across a great span as far as they could see changing in shades from light, gray-green to dark, almost black.

They came to a wide rock ledge. Kristina pushed the chair onto the level surface facing the ocean. She stood for a time letting the breeze caress and soothe, letting no thoughts creep into her mind to mar the scene that spread before them. Finally, she took the newspaper she had tucked under her arm, moved beside Anna, and lowered herself in a swift, uncomplicated way to the ledge.

She unfolded the paper. "Now, what would you like to

hear about. Who's blowing up who, or is it whom? The bleak financial outlook? Hey, here's something interesting. If you're a farmer, you can now insure your crop against acts of God like flood, frost, or drought." Kristina paused, read the words silently to herself and looked up at Anna who was staring out to sea. She studied her quietly remember the doctor's words. She had grown angry at his sanctimonious piety. . . . "We don't always understand the way of the Lord. . . ." What kind of God? A god of wrath, of vengeance? But what had Anna ever done?

Kristina had never been sure what she believed, but now she was almost sure. There was no God. How could there be? She shook herself free of her speculation and continued, "Let's see: Hogs and pork closed mixed, grains and soybeans down, potatoes down, sugar down, coffee up! Cotton depressed, wood weak." She scanned through page after page looking for a note of cheer. Reading the paper was hardly an uplifting experience. Finally she closed the paper and joined her mother in her sea gazing. Kristina breathed deeply sucking in the sounds and smells. The cry of the gulls cast a melancholy note over the scene. Spring was supposed to be filled with promise. Why did she feel so down?

Actually what she really wanted to talk to Anna about was Jill. The warmth she had felt. The way Jill had stuck up for Paul. How easy it seemed to talk to her. Anna would like Jill. Kristina was sure of that. There was something about the feel of her. Jill was one of the few people Kristina had been able to relate to in a long time.

Perhaps her reaction was in answer to a need that existed now where none had before. Her solitude had begun to weigh on her. Her lonely walks along the ocean and through the cliffs above the house no longer left her relaxed and happy but rather morose. Her moods and depressions were unfamiliar, and her ability to cope limited. If she could only talk to her father, but she really didn't know him. Anna was all Kristina had ever needed, even to the exclusion of friends her own age. She was only now beginning to realize the extent that she had depended on her mother. Was it possible that their relationship had been "unhealthy" like her father had said?

"I met this girl today, Anna." She paused waiting for her mother to respond. Anna turned and looked at her for a moment.

"That's nice." She returned to her sea gazing.

Kristina swallowed and went on. "She was different. She . . . she reminded me of you."

Anna turned back to her, her eyes narrowed studying Kristina. "Oh—was she crippled?"

"No . . ." Kristina couldn't keep the exasperation from her voice. "No, like you were before. . . ."

"Oh, you mean when I was a real person?"

It was the way she said it that made Kristina feel all twisted and angry. She clamped her lips in a thin line and turned abruptly away. The breeze off the water ruffled, lifting her hair, cooling the flush that had spread through her. Anna resumed her vigil.

"Oh never mind." Kristina rose, stretched and stared out over the water. "I wonder how cold it is?" She looked down at her mother. "If you wouldn't mind, I'll just run down and get my feet wet." She pulled the sweater up around her mother's neck. "Here, I'll turn your chair so that you can watch." She maneuvered the wheelchair onto the flat ledge. "I won't be long." She raced down the path with long strides, punctuated by scissor-quick leaps, moving out of sight beneath the steep cliffs, and then reappeared on the sand below.

Waving up to her mother, she danced out to the edge of the water and then retreated. Caught up in her usual routine, she chased the waves and was in turn chased by them.

Kristina paused momentarily, removed her sneaks, pulled

up her jeans to mid-calf, and then tiptoed out letting the waves wash around her tender feet. She leaped into the air and yelped in shock, splashing as she landed in the water. She turned to wave to Anna and stopped—all the play draining from her. Kristina rubbed her eyes and stared up at the cliff. Oh God! She had spotted her mother's chair. It was moving . . . ever so slowly toward the edge of the cliff.

She turned, leaped from the water and flew toward the path. How could it be? As she jumped the first group of rocks on the path and started to climb, she heard her father's voice, "Anna! Anna!" The harsh sound of fear wrapped itself around her throat tightening like a fist. Inside she was screaming, but she could not push the sound past her lips.

Kristina hardly felt the sharp painful stabs of loose stones and briers that cut and tore at her bare feet. She bound up the path and burst into the clearing. Her father was struggling, trying to hold Anna and the chair that had slipped precariously one wheel spinning in the air; the other lodged between a rock holding the chair momentarily as it teetered on the edge of the cliff.

She stood frozen. "Help me, Kristina! For God's sake help me." Her father's words sprang her loose from her shock and she reached over grasping the side of the chair.

7

Together they struggled, succeeding finally in dragging the chair and its occupant back to the safety of the path. Rodney Lowrey moved in behind the chair taking control pushing Kristina aside. He leaned protectively toward Anna as he began to push her back toward the house. He'd only gone a few feet when he stopped, turned to Kristina, who stood beside the path, face pale, still shaking.

"As soon as I get your mother settled, I want to talk with you, young lady." The coldness of his words slapped at her. Her trembling turned to a shudder. She watched her father as he pushed Anna toward the safety of the house, then turned and started down the path.

Wincing at the jab of a sharp stone, she looked down at the red stain of blood on her right heel and fingered gingerly the slash she had received on her wild race up the path. She didn't stop but attempted to pick her way more carefully down the path to the sea.

Kristina made her way to a large, flat rock amidst a pile of boulders. Settling herself Indian style, she cupped her chin in her hands and stared out across the water. What had happened? How could the chair have moved from where she'd placed it? She closed her eyes trying to picture the ledge. It was flat. She recalled the stone surface with the shalelike ridges that made it difficult to push the chair across it. She hadn't even thought about setting the safety latch.

"I want to talk with you, young lady." The coldness of her father's voice intruded into her thoughts. He didn't think . . . she shuddered unable to bring herself to acknowledge the thought. But, of course, it was there and she could not ignore it. How could he even consider such a possibility? She could never . . . *"You might as well be dead, might as well be dead . . . dead!"* Her hysterical words echoed over and over in her head. But she'd never . . . how could he even think she could?

Was Kristina afraid of her own father? She was surprised by her feeling of apprehension. Of course she wasn't frightened, but she was confused. Could you love someone and hate them at the same time? What kind of man was Rodney Lowrey? It was a question she had asked before and never had come up with an answer. Perhaps because until now there had been no need. No interest. No room. Oh, she knew *things* about her father. He was soft-spoken, slow to anger, and when angered was more apt to resort to sulking or sarcasm than to shouting or violence. He enjoyed solitary things like fishing, sailing, hiking, but seemed to have little time for them, at least until recently he'd spent most of his weekends in his office. There always seemed to be a *special* project with a deadline that had to be met.

When her father did socialize, he preferred people in small numbers, avoiding crowded parties or large events. He was a jazz fan enjoying Herbie Mann and Dave Brubeck over the more formal music of Chopin, Mozart, or the music of the ballet. As a matter of fact, he did not like the ballet at all, and it was only through Anna's insistence and his consideration for her that he attended Kristina's performances. She had known this for some time and had almost managed to forget that niggling sensation of . . . what was it? Hurt? Resentment? Since the accident, he had used Anna's needs as an excuse not to attend her recitals. Kristina was surprised that, under the circumstances, his attendance meant anything at all to her, but when Paul's mother had come to pick her up, there had been something strange mixed with her usual preperformance nerves.

Maybe it wasn't so much that *he* did not want to come that bothered her but rather Anna's seeming lack of interest. Since her return from the hospital, she had never once asked Kristina about her dancing. It was as if ballet had never existed. The records that she had always played: Chopin, Tchaikovsky, now lay silent. Instead, the sounds of her father's jazz echoed throughout the house. If only . . . she had hesitated at the door.

"Give a great performance," he had called from Anna's room. There was only silence from Kristina's mother.

"Yeah. Sure." She muttered and slammed the door behind her. It wasn't just hurt. It was . . . she pushed the realization away hastily. No. She could never resent Anna. After all she needed so much now.

Need. That was it. But Kristina had needs, too. Didn't her father know? Couldn't he see how lost she'd become?

In her agitation, Kristina climbed off her boulder and began pacing the beach, seeking the hard, wet sand near the water's edge. She ignored—even welcomed—the sharp stinging of the salt water. When she came upon her sneakers, she bent, picked them up, and poured the sand from them watching the fine stream drift away. Then, dropping them, she jabbed her feet into them forgetting her cuts until reminded by a sharp pain. Kristina bent, retrieved the soft heel with her forefinger, pulled the laces tight and tied them.

The echoes of her name drifted loosely on the night air. She lifted her head listening then turned and saw her father's silhouette outlined against the sky. He was standing on the ledge where she had left Anna. Kristina waved, turned and started rather doggedly up the path. The tempo of her heart increased until it was racing as much as it had on her previous wild journey.

Head down, Kristina trudged up the steep, twisting path toward her father. The sun had almost set. A fiery-orange edged the thin cirrous strips that spread outward from the sun uniting water and sky. Tall and lean he blocked the pathway. She didn't look at him immediately, instead her eyes clung stubbornly to the tip of his well-polished loafer. Reluctantly her gaze traveled upward until it settled on his face. She wanted to look away, but the grim set of his full mouth, the intensity of his narrowed eyes, the color of blue fog held her own. She noted that his hair had grown longer than usual and now curled up the nape of his neck and around his ears, a style she found more appealing than the short trim he usually wore. Upon close inspection she saw a few gray hairs, but to the casual observer, Rodney Lowrey looked much younger than his forty-seven years. If asked if he were handsome, she would have had to pause and deliberate upon the question for she rarely looked at him other than as her father.

"Well, young lady. What happened?"

"I don't know, Father. Honest. I set the chair right here on the ledge. I just wanted to go down to test the water. I hadn't been gone more than ten minutes."

He moved from the path over to the ledge and rubbed his foot along the tiny crevices of the shale rock. "How close to the edge did you put it?"

"Not that close." Kristina joined him. "I think it was about here. I was sitting reading the paper . . . " she turned and looked. "There it is." The paper had blown loose catching up in the thorny undergrowth. "When I decided to go down to the water, I turned Anna so she could watch me."

"Did you set the safety?" His eyes held hers. She wanted to look away but couldn't.

"I didn't think about it."

"Why not?" His voice was cold, impersonal.

Kristina flared hotly beneath his gaze. Her voice rose loud and shrill. "Well, look at the ledge. It's flat with all those ruts. That chair wasn't going anywhere. It couldn't just start rolling all by itself."

"It could if you put it here." He ran his foot along a smooth section of the ledge very close to the edge.

"Why would I put her way over there? She wouldn't be able to see over the mesquite down to the beach. I'm telling you, I put the chair right here so she could watch me."

"Well, then, how did it happen? I got here just before the chair toppled over the edge."

"I don't know!" She bit her lip to hold back the tears.

"You shouldn't have left her. . . . His voice was accusing. She felt the unfairness, the underlying accusation.

"I wasn't gone that long." Her voice had hardened to match his, her eyes narrowed. Anger and hurt thrashed about inside her. Just because he was willing to spend every spare moment; she hadn't been careless or neglectful. Anna hadn't complained or insisted she stay. She expected Kristina to live. Kristina swallowed at the guilt, anger and hurt that her father's insinuation had set churning.

She watched him warily as he paced back and forth. He ran his fingers through his hair that had become even curlier with the moist evening air. The fast dimming light caught at the lines around his eyes and mouth etching them deeper. Suddenly Kristina lost hold of her own misery and for a moment she felt his despair. She wanted to reach out to him, to comfort him. For the first time she realized Anna was a shared loss. In her own grief she had given little thought to all that he had lost. She started to move toward him to apologize when he stopped his pacing and turned toward her.

"If I thought for one minute . . . "

Kristina froze. Her heart stopped. Everything seemed to stand still except for the pounding surf. Their eyes met and locked. Her breath, caught up for what seemed like forever, escaped in a low hissing sound. "That I'd murder my own mother?" she whispered.

The shock of hearing a thought that neither had allowed full formation within their own minds spoken aloud was a physical blow to them both. Kristina staggered slightly from the impact. She searched her father's face for his denial to her words, and then turned sobbing, stumbling blindly down the path.

"No! Wait! Kristina! I . . . "

But she was running wildly, crying, holding her hands over her ears.

8

Jill and Kristina climbed through the ravine which had been cut through the rocky cliff by the rushing waters of small streams that swelled and diminished with seasonal rains. Stones of all shapes, sizes, and colors had been washed free and were piled loosely in various arrangements. Jill paused, stood back, head cocked to one side, studying the natural structure before her. "It's Puff the Magic Dragon riding on a flying carpet over the Matterhorn while smoking his peace pipe."

Kristina stopped still and stared at Jill's back. It was as if Anna were back and they had resumed their old game. She moved in beside Jill and studied the stone sculpture. Finally she shook her head.

"Wrong!" She said it quite emphatically.

"What do you mean, wrong? That is too Puff."

"Yeah, but that's no peace pipe."

"Oh yeah, what is it then?"

"He's trying to quit. It's one of those cigarette holders!"

"Ah, you got no imagination!" Jill turned and continued up the ravine. Kristina fell in behind her. The silence resettled comfortably.

She welcomed Jill's silence and was content to follow along letting her mind float freely as they wound their way upward into the hills. Her new friend seemed to understand the need for silence. It was the first shared solitude that she had experienced since Anna's accident. Although she had hiked alone seeking the contentment she and Anna had enjoyed, her lonely trips into the hills had only heightened her sense of loss. Jill's presence made the difference. Kristina was nearly content.

They came to a grassy knoll where Kristina plunked down on a pile of stones leaning back to rest. Jill settled into the grass that was soft and green from the recent spring rain.

"I wonder what kind of animal burrowed those holes?" Kristina mused pointing absently to a series of small indentions brown against the grass.

"Probably some Homo sapien," Jill leaned over and stuck her finger into the hole nearest her searching for something. She pulled out a small piece of root and brushed the dirt from it.

Curiosity pushed Kristina forward. "What's that? What would people be digging up around here for?"

"Soap."

"What?"

"It's a soap plant." Jill turned and looked about her. "See that plant with the leaves that look like cornstalks. The Indians call it amole or soap plant." She laughed at the disbelief on Kristina's face. "Would I kid you, Kristy?" Anna's nickname for her caught Kristina, jarring her. She started to say something then stopped. Somehow it seemed right for Jill to call her that. "You see this bulb?" Jill continued, holding up a tiny piece of root. "You peel the brown stuff off." She stripped the outer coat demonstrating, exposing a white fibrous bulb. "Mash this up and presto—soap—free for the gathering. The Mexicans and natives have used it for years."

"No kidding? What does it smell like?"

"Well, it's not Camay, but it's not bad. Here, smell it." Jill tossed Kristina the root. While she sniffed it, Jill went on. "Another little extra—after you're through washing with it in the river, you can scoop up your breakfast without ever baiting a hook. There's something in it that stuns the fish. They float to the top of the water for easy picking, like down off a goose. Of course the conservationists thought that wasn't very sporting, so now it's illegal. Mostly though, Indians weren't so concerned with the sport as they were with feeding themselves."

"How do you know all that?" Kristina narrowed her eyes, suspicious that Jill was putting her on.

"I kid you not." Jill held up her hand in an Indian salute. "Me half Paiute on my father's side. Grandfather tribal medicine man. Expert on rain dance, sun dance, spirit dance. Drive off evil spirits to make you well again!"

Kristina sat up abruptly, the amused smile gone. She leaned toward Jill. "You serious?"

"About what?"

"About your grandfather?"

"What? That he's a medicine man?"

"Yes."

"Sure, I'm serious."

Kristina studied Jill thoughtfully. "Would he come see my mother?"

"What's the matter with your mother?"

"Everything." Kristina moved from her pile of stones and joined Jill in the grass. She pulled up a tender green shoot and chewed on it as she gazed off into the distance. Jill waited. A patient sort of silence, not uncomfortable, grew between them. When Kristina started to talk, the words poured freely, like water from a broken dam.

Jill let loose a long, low whistle. "Gosh, Kristy, I'm sorry."

Kristina brushed at the sympathy impatiently like a cobweb across her face. "Would he come?"

"Hey, he's not a witch doctor. He can't walk on water. He's just an old Indian who knows a lot about the healing plants that grow around here, how to treat snake bites, stuff like that."

"Has he ever helped anyone who was crippled?"

"Well . . ." Jill wouldn't look at her. She picked at the small root in her hand. Kristina's eagerness heightened with her silence.

"He has, hasn't he?"

"Gosh, Kristy, it probably wasn't anything like your mother. I mean not anything so serious."

"But that's it. Maybe it's some little thing that the other doctors have overlooked. Some tiny, little—will he come?"

"I don't know. He really doesn't do a lot of doctoring anymore. Hardly ever makes any potions . . . just a few for old friends. He probably wouldn't."

"Would you ask him? I mean if he'd just come and talk to Anna about plants. She's really into that sort of thing . . . or at least she was. She'd love it. I know."

"Well . . ." Jill looked dubious. "I don't know. I'll ask."

"You'll really try, won't you? I mean to persuade him. We'd pay."

"Oh you couldn't do that! Grandfather says you can't take money for driving out evil spirits. Ruins the vibes or something."

Kristina was up dusting off the seat of her pants. The two girls resumed their slow meandering along the path. The hills were fresh and green, smelling of new growth. Kristina breathed deeply. She felt light. The world was beautiful. Wild daisies swayed in the light breeze. Out across the slopes were large patches of yellow buttercups. The mauve lupine spikes were everywhere; she threw her arms wide as if to catch the breeze and hug it.

"Look!" She pointed to the silent swooping, soaring of a

large hawk dark against the sky. They stood, heads thrown back, watching as the bird rose effortlessly, soaring, and riding the wind. "That's what I'd like to be." Kristina's voice was filled with admiration as she watched the bird maneuvering itself using only its shape and form as it rolled and dipped. "It's so perfect; the way things are supposed to be." Suddenly the bird tucked its wings close and knifed earthward into a steep dive. Just before it hit the ground, the hawk spread its wings, extended its sharp claws and plucked up a small rodent that had been hiding among the loose stones. Flapping its wings lazily, the bird rose. The shrill screams of the rodent spread in widening circles.

Kristina sucked in her breath. Stooping, she picked up a handful of rocks and started yelling and chasing the hawk throwing rocks at its climbing form. "Come on, Jill, we've got to save it!" But it was no use. The two girls stood staring after the shrinking form of the hawk. The thin squealing echoed. "The poor thing. If only I could have helped."

Jill shrugged. "Don't be silly. There're some things you can change and there're some things you can't. The hawk has to live too."

"But the poor mouse. He wasn't doing anything."

Jill looked at Kristina curiously. "But that's the way it is. Life's not all soaring you know."

Kristina said nothing. Jamming her hands deep into her pockets, she stared into the emptiness the hawk had left.

"If we didn't have hawks and things to eat mice, we'd be overrun with them. Then we'd have to poison or trap them. This is cleaner. Nature's way."

"It's very cruel, isn't it." It wasn't a question, rather an observation. Kristina looked down at the ground then kicked viciously at a loose stone. The beauty was gone. She reached down, unthinking, and picked a leaf from a vine that crawled rampantly over the underbrush. She started to chew on it.

"Don't do that!" Jill slapped her hand away from her mouth.

"What . . . " Anger flashed across Kristina's face.

"I'm sorry, I didn't mean to hit you, but you shouldn't go around putting leaves in your mouth. They could kill you. Especially that!"

Kristina looked at the light green foliage studded with tiny, starlike flowers. "What is it?"

"It's called big root or wild cucumber. I'm not sure about the leaves, all I know is that grandfather says the potion from the seeds is deadly."

"Well, if it's so poisonous, what would they be making potions out of it for?"

"They don't anymore."

"What did they use it for?"

"Just for the hopeless cases. To help the old and sick die easier."

"Your grandfather poisoned people?"

Jill bristled. "I don't think grandfather ever did. But when someone is hopelessly sick, I mean when they don't want to live." Jill groped for the right words and then shrugged. "It's like shooting a horse with a broken leg."

Kristina tensed. "Mercy killing?"

"I guess that's what you'd call it."

"You think that's okay?"

"If you're old, or there's no hope, I mean who'd want to just lie around and have people take care of you?"

Kristina bent and fingered the leaf gently. "What did you call it?"

"Big root. Its root is supposed to be as big as a barrel."

"How do they make the potion?"

"I don't know. Grandfather doesn't share all his secrets."

"But he never used it?"

"That's it. No one knows for sure. There aren't any symptoms."

58

"Is it painful?"

"Hey, why the third degree? You planning on doing someone in or something?"

"Of course not!" Kristina turned abruptly and started back down the ravine.

"Hey, wait! No need to get huffy." Jill hurried after her.

9

The girls picked their way down the ravine in silence. Not
the same comfortable silence they had before, but an edgy
absence of speech that tumbled between them like a loose
stone dislodged from the creek bed. When they arrived at
the bottom, Kristina turned toward home.

"Hey." Jill reached out for her. "Can't you come to my
house for a while? We can bake some cookies or something.
I'll fill you in on the latest ghost story." Jill's smile did odd
things with her face . . . something that warmed Kristina. It
wasn't anything you could describe, but rather something
you felt. She hesitated then returned the smile.

"Sure . . . if it's chocolate chip and the stories are sexy."
The girls reached out to one another and it was all right
again. They turned down the path that led to Jill's house.

With a plate of warm cookies between them, the soft
strains of a western ballad echoing of mountains and streams,
the girls lay on the floor. Together, yet separate. Listening.

"Have you ever been . . . well . . . sorry or ashamed that
you're part Indian?" Kristina had rolled over and was studying Jill. "I mean do you ever hate white people?"

Jill did not move but continued lying studying the ceiling.
Silence hung momentarily, a silence that Kristina had come
to expect, for Jill rarely answered a serious question without
slow consideration. She rolled over, propped her chin in her

hand, and gazed long and hard at Kristina. She began to pluck at the rug with methodical deliberation.

"It's not something you think of in your head. Rather it's something you feel right here." Jill held her fist against her stomach. "I can't describe it, but when I go visit my grandfather on the reservation, I see it in his eyes. It's not that he's bitter, but there's something there. A lost, haunted look. He's such a proud man, and then I feel it's not pity. I could never pity a man like Pioto, but it's like looking at a man who was intended to do great deeds and was never allowed. Like a runner confined to a leash, or an eagle that has been made into a pet and kept in a cage."

"But," Kristina spoke tensely. "Why did he allow it to happen? I mean if he really wanted and needed something, if he'd have really tried . . . " She sat up abruptly and swung her legs in front of her crossing them Indian syle.

Jill stopped her plucking at the rug. She narrowed her eyes and studied Kristina. Finally she shrugged and rolled over on her back. "Why didn't the mouse escape the hawk? That's the way it is."

"No!" It was a sharp denial. "It's not like that. If you try hard enough . . . "

"Oh, Kristy, be realistic. There are some things you just can't change . . . except maybe a record." She jumped up from the floor and started going through her stack. She chose a group with a sensuous rock sound, put it on the stereo, threw her head back, and began to snap her fingers. Slowly, rhythmically, she began to dance. Kristina watched her friend . . . hair, a wispish, fine halo; eyes closed. Jill could be a great ballerina. She had the subtlety, the feeling. Like Anna. Kristina rose. She joined Jill, loosing herself in the music.

With another batch of cookies in the oven the conversation turned to teachers, students, school activities; but for some reason, Kristina kept thinking of Jill's grandfather.

"Does he visit you often?" The question popped out in the midst of a discussion of the horrors of Herman Melville's lengthy sentence structure. Without asking who, Jill responded.

"No. He doesn't come off the reservation much any more. The pollution gets him. They say it's emphysema, but he calls it white man's poison fog."

"Does he still practice his medicine?"

"Oh he helps some of the old people who come to him with little things, but he has retired from performing the life and death rituals: the old ceremonies that could only be performed if the signs were right. He says the gods are lost to him now that the world is so noisy. Claims they can't hear his chants." Jill paused, studying Kristina in that special way she had. The timer on the stove buzzed and she busied herself removing the cookies.

"He's given me one of his medicine bags. Want to see some of his tools?"

The way Jill handled the small worn leather bag made Kristina aware how special it was . . . something rarely shared like her own India box. The two girls sat crosslegged in the middle of Jill's bedroom floor. She reached into the bag and one by one arranged an assortment of strange looking objects on the carpet in front of her. There were bleached white bones and teeth, a dried snake skin, and an empty turtle shell.

Kristina watched and listened to Jill who, almost trance-like, recited the special powers of each item. Of them all, Kristina became most fascinated with a smooth, milky stone that caught the light, reflecting it softly in a strange, hypnotic way. Jill's voice droned on, but she saw only the stone. She reached out hesitantly and then pulled back only to reach for it again.

"What is it?" Her question interrupted Jill's recitation.

"The moonstone?"

"May I hold it?"

Without a word Jill picked it up and handed it to her. She took it almost reverently. It lay in the palm of her hand glowing softly. "What is a moonstone?"

Jill hesitated. "It's a special stone that is supposed to glow and dull with the waxing and waning of the moon."

Kristina continued to stare at the stone cradled softly in her hand. Jill paused. Kristina looked up studying her friend intently. She sensed her hesitation.

Jill waved her hand carelessly. "There's some old legend that it will see the soul safely from one world to the next. Grandfather believes the spirit can get lost and end up wandering about the earth like a displaced person. Kind of like our ghost here in the house."

Kristina continued to stare at the moonstone. "Could I have it?" Her voice was barely a whisper.

"Well . . ." Jill hesitated, "I . . ."

"I'm sorry." Kristina shook her head slightly and thrust the stone back at Jill. 'It's your grandfather's."

"I promised, I mean when he gave me his bag, that I'd keep his things forever." Jill took the stone and held it for a moment running her finger over its smooth, milky surface. "And there are those rare occasions when he comes visiting. He sometimes takes his things up into the hills behind us. I've never gone with him, but I think he performs the ancient chants and ceremonies. Relives the old days. It's all he has and . . ."

"Forget it, Jill. I shouldn't have asked. Hey, what about the cookies?" Kristina jumped up and headed for the kitchen.

10

Kristina stood uneasily shifting her weight first on one leg and then the other. There were seven of them, all female: three teenagers, a couple of young housewives, and two older women. The antiseptic smell made her nose twitch, and the bells and voices droning over the loud speaker, calling first one doctor and then another, swelled and ebbed almost as constantly as the waves that rolled upon the beach in front of her house.

It was a dumb idea. What good could she do? She had thought volunteering at the hospital might make it easier with Anna, but now, standing there uneasily, she had to suppress the urge to turn and run. Kristina forced her attention back to the nurse who was explaining the needs of the different areas of the hospital and asking the volunteers if they had a preference.

She swallowed and raised her hand. "I would like to work with the crippled children."

"Good, that's one area where we really need help." She noted something on her pad and continued questioning other volunteers. Satisfied at last, she proceeded with hospital information regarding hours, parking, and instruction available to the volunteers.

Kristina followed the young nurse through a low tunnel-like corridor. People moved past them like robots, not smiling or greeting. An old man dressed in a shapeless white gown supported himself on a frame that rolled on wheels. Each shaky, tentative step he took was achieved with such total concentration that he was oblivious of his surroundings.

She was not prepared. The only children she had ever known were normal and active. She could not help but draw back from what she saw. Children of various ages milled about the room. Some were in braces, others unable to sit alone were propped with support. One little boy was so cross-eyed it pained her to look at him. The knot in her chest grew tighter. The nurse, oblivious, continued to introduce her patients to Kristina and then softly explained each one's problem. She did it so matter-of-factly, with no sense of emotion.

She went on introducing, explaining, but Kristina had ceased to listen. Instead, she watched a small baby in a crib near her. He looked so perfect. Surely there was nothing serious. "Billy Lowder, six months, severe brain damage at birth. Prospects for walking, talking..." The nurse's voice was caught in the crevices of her mind. His eyes were a deep blue. He smiled, made baby noises, and flung his arms about. They must be wrong. He looked so perfect. The shadow of Anna, of what she had been, fell across Billy and Kristina could not hold back the tears. It wasn't fair! It was horrible! It all caught up in her. She turned blindly and ran.

If he hadn't been so strong, they both would have been sprawled full-length across the shiny, slick floor; but he held her firmly until they had regained their balance.

"Hey, hold on. What's the problem?"

Kristina looked up into brown eyes with tiny sunburned lines etched about them. His hair was streaked blond, his skin a coppery tan. Mostly she was aware of his hands. Firm, and yet, even while they held her securely, there was a gentleness about them. She felt a shock of excitement surge through her at his touch and for a moment the misery that had overwhelmed her was forgotten.

"Why the tears?"

It came rushing back. She had meant to keep it all to herself, but there was something about him. "I . . . Billy . . . he seems so perfect and there's no hope. It's so awful. At least Anna . . ." At that point she broke down completely. The sobs piled up until they finally burst out. He held her against him, not trying to stop her crying, comforting her without words. All the tears she had been holding back, the misery of the past months now washed through her. The release left Kristina drained. She clung to him needing his strength. He continued to hold her as her sobs slowed from great rushing waves to shallow hiccups and finally to an occasional sigh. Gradually, she became aware of the people moving around them in the narrow hall, of their curious stares.

Embarrassed, Kristina pulled away from him wiping at her eyes with the back of her hand snuffling hard like a small child. What a sight she must be! She couldn't bring herself even to look at him. Still not speaking, he handed her his handkerchief. She accepted it gratefully relieved to have something to mop her face with.

Why did she have to cry? She couldn't find words to describe the swelling of her eyes or her round, red nose. For Kristina crying was worse than a bad case of hives. Her face puffed up with red-and-white blotches, her nose didn't drip, it ran profusely, and her eyes not only swelled to mere slits but became bloodshot.

"I'm sorry." Her words were a low, husky whisper; her eyes never left the tip of her loafers as she continued mopping at her face, and then there was no getting around it; she had to blow her nose. She tried to do it quietly, a tiny little snuff, but it was no use. Finally she let loose and blew. A resounding honking echoed through the hall.

"That'a girl!" His words were approving, supporting like the warmth of his hands that continued to pat her on the shoulder. "I was just on my way to the cafeteria for a break. How about keeping me company?" He didn't wait for an answer but propelled her down the hall toward the elevator. "I'm Doctor Feldman. David."

Kristina twisted the straw between her fingers. She stared unseeing into the dark, bubbly coke. Her words, hesitant at first, became strong and clear. "It's not just Billy. I guess it's mostly my mother." She paused looking up at him. He held his coffee cup in the hollow of one hand sipping the hot liquid. Although he said nothing she was encouraged. "You should have known her—Annya." The name slipped unbidden from her lips and echoed in Kristina's mind. Although she was looking at a young blond man, she was seeing the slim, eager woman her mother had been. She slipped back, something she had not allowed herself to do for a long time. She and her mother were together once more sharing, growing, loving. Echoes of laughter, whispers of questions, the feel of her hand in Anna's.

"What happened?"

They were at the bar practicing fouettés.

"Was it an accident?"

They were racing through the surf.

It was the touch of his hand on her arm that brought Kristina back to her coke, the cafeteria, and David Feldman. She looked at him blankly. "Your mother, was it an accident?"

She stared down into the blackness of her drink and began stabbing at the ice cubes with her straw. "It was seven months ago." She paused turning the figure over in her mind. *Only seven months ago?* Her echo was a question.

"Sometimes I think she'd be better off dead." Her words were flat, emotionless. "You'll think I'm awful just like my father does, but I know Anna, or I used to." She looked at him studying him for a long moment and then finished lamely, "I just know."

She had been on the verge of telling him how close she and her mother had been, but when she tried, everything seemed just out of her grasp. What she wanted to share had become vague and distant, an elusive memory that refused to take form in her mind. She finally gave up and went on. "The doctors say there's not much hope of her ever getting any better. Just like little Billy." She paused waiting for him to deny what she had concluded. He said nothing. "I shouldn't have come. I thought..." She twisted the straw jamming it through the ice, "I could learn, could understand, could accept, even help. I can't. All I can do is cry. What possible pleasure can that baby ever get out of life?" She leaned forward searching his eyes for the answer but didn't wait. "He'll never be able to walk, to skate, to..." she searched for the word, "to fly..." she finished lamely.

"That's where you're wrong." His voice was warm, quiet. The cafeteria noises went almost unnoticed. He reached out to Kristina taking her hand in his. He examined it carefully running his fingers along her palm, turning it over tracing the smoothness of her young fingers, noting the clean, perfect shape of her nails. Then he covered it with his own. "Could you live without this hand?"

She jerked it back from him curling her fingers into a fist as if testing its strength. She held her hand close rubbing it with the other. "Well..."

"Of course you could. What would it take... six months? A year? To forget what it was to have two hands. You'd learn to do everything with your other hand: eat, write, throw. It would grow stronger, more agile. That is our hope . . . that we can retrain Billy's brain to compensate for what has been damaged. It's true. With what we know today Billy is doomed to a life like the one you described. But we are learning every day. Already we have been able to help people to adjust, to compensate for their losses." He looked at her, searching her face. "We're all crippled someway. It's just more obvious in some than others. For some of us it's easier, and we must help those less fortunate."

Kristina wanted to look away, but he compelled her with his eyes. There was something about him. He reached out taking her hand again. His warmth flowed through her. "We hope," he said softly. She could feel the tears starting all over, but he didn't give them a chance, "and work like hell!" He pulled her to her feet. "Come on, I'll show you a few giant strides we've made."

Kristina watched him with the children. When he came into the room, all became aware of his presence. Those that could, moved to him holding up their hands to be picked up and held, which he did with great enthusiasm. All except one little girl who Kristina judged to be about five years old. She remained quietly in the corner, her legs encased in the steel spines of braces. She did not look up or smile at him the way the other children did but remained sullen, head down, eyes glued to the tips of her toes. Kristina felt her chest tightening again with pity. She was such a pretty girl, deep red hair like her own, creamy white complexion, and already her features were emerging into the shadowy silhouette of what she would someday become. What had happened? David came up to Kristina. It was as if he'd heard her inner question.

"It was an auto accident," he explained quietly. "She went through the windshield. She can't walk. Doesn't speak either, but we aren't sure whether that is physical or psychosomatic. Come, let me introduce you." He lead Kristina over to the small figure.

The child did not look up at him, but continued to stare at her toes. He reached out and took her hand much like he had Kristina's. "Allison?" She looked up. Kristina sucked in her breath startled by the intense violet color of her eyes. "I want you to meet Kristina." Her eyes shifted slowly to Kristina. It wasn't the vacant stare of a mindless person, but rather disinterest until she saw Kristina's hair so much like her own. For a moment there was a spark of interest and then Allison returned to staring at the braces attached to her legs.

"Those braces are to help you, Allison. They'll make it so you can walk again." Ther was no response to his words. He remained kneeling by her side. He reached out and smoothed her hair running his fingers through it gently. "Good-bye, Allison. I'll stop and see you tomorrow." He rose and moved away. Kristina followed.

He studied the forlorn little figure from across the room. "Her mother brings her here hoping the other children will stimulate her into some sort of response. She's been here off and on several weeks now, but we haven't made much progress. Actually she's nowhere near ready for those braces, but we put them on so that she can see them and get used to them. We were hoping they'd spark her into some kind of action. We're trying everything."

"How long ago was the accident?" Kristina couldn't take her eyes off the small figure huddled in the corner.

"Six months. The damage was to the motor nerves. They have not been totally destroyed though, because she can move her hands some and we think maybe there is some motion in the arms. We hope . . ." his voice died as he too studied Allison, "and work like hell!"

Kristina turned to him. "I wasn't going to come back. I still don't know if I can help, but I want to try. Do you think . . ."

she hesitated dropping her eyes, "I mean I know you're busy," she looked up at him again and rushed on, "but could you come see my mother?"

He studied her for a moment. "You realize I'm just an intern here. I'm not . . . "

"Just a visit. Nothing professional. Just meet her . . . please." She tried to hide the urgency in her voice. Kristina was unaware of how hard she was squeezing his hand.

"Well, that depends."

"On what?"

"If I'll need corrective surgery on my right hand when you get through."

"Oh! I'm sorry." She dropped his hand blushing a bright crimson. "You will come . . . as a friend?"

"As a friend, I'll be glad to."

11

"Will your folks let you go alone?" Kristina was excited by Jill's idea of backpacking into a camping area on Cape Lookout.

"I wouldn't be alone. I'd be with you."

"You know what I mean. No adults. My father's always pretty strict. He probably won't think it's safe."

"The camp's supervised. There's always a ranger around. Besides, who's going to bother us? Most campers are people just like you and me out to enjoy nature. There're all kinds of trails, beaches, forests. We could picnic on the beach, maybe even sleep there if we're sneaky enough."

"Why would we have to sneak?"

"Rules."

"What if we get caught?"

"Well, it's no federal offense. They probably won't throw us in jail."

"I don't have any camping gear."

"We've got lots. You can use Mom's; she won't mind."

"How'd we get there?"

"Mom could drive us up on Friday after school and pick us up on Sunday."

"What if it rains?"

"So we get a little wet." Jill threw up her hands in exasperation. "Boy, are you the cautious one! They have telephones you know. We can always call if we want to leave early. We'll play it by ear."

Jill's idea voiced such a short time ago had already taken hold of her imagination. A whole weekend of hiking through sand dunes and fern grottoes, of seeing wild animals, and of sitting by a camp fire on the beach with Jill. If they were lucky, and the weather stayed warm, but would her father let her go? Before the accident she would not even have considered asking him, she would go to Anna. But now . . .

Kristina took the list Jill had given her. Already she was checking to see if she had everything. She knew that she should talk to her father first, but she went on checking the list: canteen, food (canned and dried), clothing (light weight, multiple layers for protection against wind and dampness), toothbrush, hiking shoes. All Kristina had were sneaks which would have to do even though Jill said they weren't as good as hiking boots. Some dry socks, and . . . Kristina fingered her bathing suit. Silly. It was too early. The water would be freezing. She pushed it back into the drawer. Besides, a lot of the beaches were closed to swimming.

Jill was going to provide a sleeping bag, tent, cooking utensils, and backpacks. She was also getting the permit. The more Kristina thought about it, the more eager she became. She needed to get away from—it was a terrible thought but she couldn't help it—she needed to get away from Anna.

All she had to do now was to convince her father to let her go. She sighed. That wasn't going to be easy. Kristina took a deep breath and knocked lightly on her father's door.

"Come in."

She hesitated. For a moment she wanted to turn and run, but then she straightened her shoulders and pushed open the door. He sat at his drafting table working on some sketches. He didn't look up immediately but continued filling in details. She stood inside the door watching his quick, sure movements.

He paused, looked up and then straightened on his stool. "Come in, Kristina. Just finishing up a few details on J. B.'s house. What do you think?"

She moved across the room and looked over his drawings. The house sketched before her was much more austere than their own with cubes, squares, and angles that somehow managed to be all drawn together by a strong central feeling. It resembled some of the rock sculptures she and her mother used to imagine in different shapes and creatures.

She continued to study the drawing thoughtfully. "I could learn to like it I think."

Her father was not displeased with her reaction.

"It's not beautiful like ours, but there's strength and . . . " she searched for the right word, "durability . . . no . . . longevity . . . no . . . "

"Continuity?" he suggested.

"Yeah. That's it."

"Well, I hope J. B. is as astute as you are, young lady." He leaned back and looked at her. It was an unhurried look, and for once she felt that he really saw her and that he seemed pleased with what he saw. It was a rare feeling that flooded through her. The approval she saw in his eyes warmed her and for a moment she forgot what she had come for.

"What can I do for you, kitten?"

He hadn't called her that in a long time. Suddenly she felt shy and awkward. "Jill asked me to go camping this weekend," she blurted out, "up at Cape Lookout." She rushed on. "We'd have to backpack in, but the campgrounds are all supervised. You have to get a permit and the weather's supposed to be good and I sure would like to go." So much for her prepared speech.

"What would you use for equipment?"

"Oh, Jill said I could use . . . " Kristina started to say Jill's mother's and caught herself. She continued trying to make an effort to control the pitch of her voice, "some of hers. They have lots."

"Who'd be taking you?"

"Jill's mother." She knew her father was asking one thing and she was answering another.

"Sounds like a great idea. Wish I could come, too, but . . . " he paused looking past her out through the window. "Some other time maybe." He picked up his pencil and started drawing in more details. He paused, "When would you leave?"

"Friday, right after school, and we'd be back Sunday afternoon."

"What about homework?"

"I'm all caught up. No more homework, just reviews for finals."

"Sounds good. Be careful not to swim off the point. You know that undertow."

"We will."

"Tell Mrs. Hangtree to beware of the sand fleas."

Kristina bit her lower lip. "Fath—" Just then the telephone rang.

"J. B. Yes, I have them right here." He reached for the drawings giving Kristina a small shrug.

She turned, hesitated for a moment, and then left the room closing the door behind her. She leaned against it listening to the sounds of his voice. She struggled briefly with the sin of omission then shrugged. It really didn't matter. He'd have let her go either way.

The weather turned unseasonably hot. Kristina squirmed in her seat unable to settle down to any sort of studying. Jill's whispering countdown of the remaining minutes hardly helped. It wasn't only Kristina. The restlessness of the entire class hung over the room like something physical. Finally the teacher gave up on class discussion and assigned some silent reading.

When the bell rang, she and Jill were the first ones out of their seats and through the door. "Let's go!" Jill tore down the hall with Kristina hot on her heels.

"Hey you two! No running!"

Kristina slowed to a fast walk, but Jill tore on unheeding. When she got to her locker, Jill was there tapping her foot impatiently. She waited while Kristina got her things and then they were out the main door and down the steps.

"There she is. Come on." Jill cut across the grass and was opening the door to their station wagon.

"You have everything?" Jill's mother stood before the pile of equipment stacked almost knee high. "How are you ever going to hike in with all this?"

"Don't worry, Ma, we'll make it easy. Won't we, Kristy?"

"Well . . ." she hesitated, "if you say so."

They pulled up before a small white building. Jill jumped from the car. "Come on, we'll check in."

"You did get the reservation and the permit and . . ."

"Yeah. Yeah. I took care of it. Come on."

"Just one minute, young lady. How about where and when I pick you up?"

"That's right" Jill paused. "How about right here, Sunday at four; unless you hear otherwise? Okay?" Jill turned directing her question to Kristina.

"Okay." She nodded.

"How far did you say Wild Deer Camp was?" Kristina sat on a pile of stone allowing her pack to slip from her shoulders.

"It's only four miles."

"How far do you think we've come?"

"Oh, it's not much farther. Probably a mile." Kristina had removed her shoes and was wiggling her toes through the thin, hot layer of sand down to the cool, damp surface beneath.

"Wow, is it hot! Must be almost ninety and no wind at all."

"Wait till the tide changes. That'll cool it off."

"Oh, I don't mind the heat. Actually it's neat to be hot. There's something that I can't explain about being all warm and oozy with sweat. Kind of primeval. It's good for you, too." Kristina rubbed her hand over her exposed shoulders. "I'm glad I remembered to wear a halter. Just think how tan we'll be."

"You're beginning to get red. How about me?" Jill turned and tried to peer down her own back. "I don't want to get burned."

"You're right. I guess we'd better cover up." They untied the shirts knotted about their waists and slipped them on tying them high about their midriffs.

"As soon as we pitch the tent, we'll make for the beach. Should be low tide. They got the neatest tidal pools. Maybe we can catch some crab or clams for dinner."

"Did you bring a net?"

"No, but we can make do. I have some hooks and line. We can scrounge a stick for a pole."

"I thought you had to net crabs."

"Na. We can use some mussels on a hook for bait. Crabs aren't too smart. We can flip them in." Jill demonstrated with an imaginary pole and line.

"How'll we cook them? I didn't bring a pan."

"Questions, questions. We'll figure out something."

The sound of acid rock filled the air. The girls looked back the way they'd come. Two boys walked into the opening. Both were dressed in thin, frayed jean shorts with no shirts.

They had been exposed to the sun much longer than Jill or Kristina. Already their skin had become a deep, tender looking red. Kristina winced remembering some of her own bad burns.

"Well . . . hello there."

There was something about the way he said it that made Kristina's skin crawl. Both boys had stopped close to where the girls sat. For a moment only the raspy sound of the cheap pocket radio blaring and their breathing in soft gulping snorts hung in the air. The way they continued to eye them made Kristina glad she and Jill had put on their shirts.

The one that had spoken was thin, almost scrawny. His ribs protruded like rounded washboards. His hair, probably a shade of blond when clean, now hung dark and limp pulled into a thin, greasy ponytail held by a piece of dirty, knotted toweling. Numerous long, scraggly hairs edged his rather sharp chin giving him a peculiar old-man quality. His eyes darted from Jill to Kristina.

"You two girls out here camping all by yourselves?" He moved closer, squatting very near Kristina. The smell of him pushed at her. She flushed and drew back. Her hand went protectively to her pack.

"Ye—I mean . . ."

"No." Jill interrupted, her voice calm. "Our parents are up ahead. We just got a little tired."

He turned his head slowly studying Jill. She didn't blink an eye or turn away from his scrutiny but returned his stare. He finally turned back to Kristina who had managed to inch away from him. A slow smile pulled his thin lips back exposing sharp yellowish teeth. His eyes became tiny slits and Kristina knew that her flustered stuttering had given them away.

"Hey, Buller, why don't we give these little ladies a hand with these heavy old packs?" The boy with the radio ambled forward. Kristina turned and watched him lumber his way slowly, methodically, toward the boy squatting near her. He was a mountain. Not fat. A football coach's dream. His dark hair created a kinky halo framing an expressionless, smooth face. His bulk accented the other's wiriness.

"We don't need any help from you." Both boys turned to Jill who had got up and was slipping her arms through her pack straps.

Kristina jumped to her feet reaching for her own pack. The boy who had been squatting in front of her snatched it as he stood up.

"I can manage." She wished Jill's voice hadn't been quite so cutting. Kristina reached for her pack, but he pulled it away.

"Wouldn't dream of letting little ol' you carry this heavy old thing all that way."

"Give it back." Jill's voice was even sharper than before, a tone Kristina had never heard her use before.

He turned to Jill, his eyes narrowing, his lips pulled back across his teeth into a sinister grin. Kristina reached out and snatched her pack, moving quickly across the clearing next to Jill. The smile disappeared from his face. The muscles along his jaw tightened into thin cords. He started to move toward the girls when voices drifted over the sounds of Buller's radio.

"Hello!" Three small children raced into the opening followed by their parents.

Instinctively Kristina and Jill moved toward the children. The two boys stood their ground only for a moment, and then, turning to Buller, the thin one drawled, "Let's go." Before leaving he turned, deliberately eyed Kristina up and down, and then lifted his hand in a wave. "See you later." It was a casual remark, but Kristina's skin crawled as if he had touched her.

12

As they hiked together to the camp grounds, the sun, the sound of the surf, and the laughter of the children dulled the fear she had felt. It was just her imagination!

Kristina and Jill set about selecting a campsite. The smell of the hot sun on the new undergrowth, the feel of the soft pine needle carpet, the wild rhododendrons in full bloom, all made it very difficult to decide. Each site had something different to offer. Finally they agreed upon a site high up on a ridge overlooking the ocean yet protected against the chilling western breeze by a thick row of shrubs that had woven a natural windbreak.

Kristina watched Jill skillfully assemble the tent poles and anchors. It was a small two-sleeper. Just big enough to contain their sleeping bags and packs. Then she walked around the site several times before deciding.

"Here, we'll pitch it here. It's nice and flat yet high enough for good drainage."

"What do we need good drainage for?"

"In case it rains. We don't want to wake up all soggy."

"Oh."

"Here. You take the shovel." Jill reached into her pack and withdrew a small shovel with a folded handle. She unscrewed a wing nut, straightened the handle, and tightened it again. "Dig a shallow trench along here away from the tent."

Kristina looked up at the deep blue sky that hung over them. "You expecting rain?"

"Never know. An ounce of prevention, you know." This was a whole new side of Jill. Different from the devil-may-care spontaneous Jill who jumped in to defend Paul or ignored the no-running commands.

"Now who's being cautious!" Kristina held up her hand silencing Jill's protest. "I know. . . . Be prepared!" She bent to the task all the while watching Jill as she pitched the tent.

"There." The two of them stood back admiring the taut yellow skin of their new house. It was silly, but Kristina couldn't help feeling a little proud. She took a bough she'd found beneath a nearby fir and brushed the ground around the front of the tent. "That should do it." She said it as if she had just accomplished a dramatic decorating job.

"Come on, let's hit the beach." They took one last look at their tent, tied the flaps against intrusion and started toward the trail.

The sun had dropped quite low creating long, thin shadows through the trees. The air, which still remained unusually warm, was not yet filled with the damp fog that crept in with the evening tides during the spring season.

The girls plunged recklessly down the shadowed trail, pausing only momentarily on the edge of the flower-strewn pasture. Even their final descent down the steep cliff was taken like two agile monkeys using the twisted shrubs to grasp, swinging themselves from one narrow outcropping to another.

Breathless, they paused, removed their shoes and on pale, tender feet raced across the sandy beach to the cold wet surf. Kristina yelped and retreated from the swirling, white froth that rushed at her. Her feet tingled with the cold and then began to ache.

"Sissy!" Jill shrieked and went further into the waves. They continued up the beach walking quietly now; their exhiliration having settled with the sun. It had been a nice sunset. Slow to color, but like a Roman candle that sputtered and belched in the beginning it had finally let loose and ended in a burst of orange and pink that had all but faded. The beach had been almost empty except for an occasional shell collector, a woman and her dog that splashed into the icy water retrieving sticks, and a family whose children raced in and out of the water squealing their pleasure. They were all gone now. Only Kristina and Jill walked the water's edge. Each was quiet, wrapped in her own thoughts, enjoying the solitude.

"Look." Jill held out her arm stopping Kristina. She pointed to a pile of driftwood huge and grotesque against the shadowed dusk. A lone figure's slow, lithe movements seemed caught in silhouette. In a vague, impressionistic way the dancer had captured the rhythm of the surf, the last trails of color in the sky, even the briny smell. As the girls watched, the dancer stood poised, the merest suggestion of movement and then he spun and leaped bringing them all together in one great crescendo—dancer, girls, sky, surf, all molded into one. The spell was broken when the figure took a deep, sweeping bow.

Jill began to applaud and Kristina joined her yelling, "Bravo, Paul. Bravo!" for she had danced too many years beside him not to recognize Paul's leaps and turns.

He stiffened at their calls and applause.

"How do you know who it is?" Jill whispered.

"It's Paul Rolland. I'd know him anywhere. Remember . . . Looney Tunes. Come on down, Paul," Kristina called. "It's just Jill and me."

The figure remained still for a moment and then began to pick his way down through the jumble of logs. Kristina tensed. She really wanted Jill to like Paul. Not to see hm as Looney Tunes the way the others did. Night had darkened the sky. The stars were bright pinpoints against the black. She could not see him clearly, so she reached out for his hand.

"Hello, Kristina."

She didn't wait for him to say anything else, but rushed her words so that they tumbled out all together. "You remember Jill? We're camping here. What are you doing here? Are your folks with you?" And then she had to stop to catch her breath. She bit her lip waiting for his usual high cackle, but only the sound of the surf and Jill's low chuckle echoed.

"Hello, Paul. That was a beautiful dance. I felt so . . . almost part of it. I hope our sharing it didn't spoil it for you."

Kristina braced herself again waiting for his Bugs Bunny imitation. Instead he released her hand and turned to Jill. He smiled broadly and bowed formally. "Spoil it? How could a performance ever be spoiled by an audience? We love it. Don't we, Kristina?"

"W-welll, yes," she stuttered. She stared at him. He seemed so relaxed.

"I'm camping here by myself. It's one of my favorite spots."

"I didn't know you liked camping." She didn't give him a chance to comment, but turned to Jill. "Hey, I'm starved. What do we have to eat besides dried soup? It's going to take gallons of that to fill me up."

"I was going to start a fire down here on the beach and fix something," Paul volunteered. "If—"

"We'll help." Jill's voice was eager. "That is if you don't mind. We can pool our supplies. Only we're warning you, we didn't bring much."

Kristina watched the two of them, heads close, laughing, talking, working with each other as if they'd done this very thing together thousands of times. She couldn't get over

Paul. He was so different, so relaxed. Jill liked him, she could tell, and she should be pleased. That was what she wanted, wasn't it? So why that funny tight feeling in her chest? It had been nicer when it was just her and Jill. Now she felt like a fifth wheel, one that was flat at that. She kicked at the sand, shoved her hands deep into her pockets and was about to walk down the beach when Paul called to her.

"Kristina, we'll need some rocks about the size of your fist. Think you can find some?"

"Sure." She started down the beach toward the mouth of a small stream she and Jill had waded through earlier.

"Hey, wait!" He called. "You'll need something to carry them in." He came up close to her in the darkness and handed her a small plastic bucket. She could even feel the difference. He seemed so sure of himself. She thought she knew him. Suddenly it occurred to her that she and Jill might have barged in on him. Maybe he came out here to be alone.

"I hope you don't mind."

"Mind what?"

"Us. I mean we did practically invite ourselves, especially to your evening meal."

"Hey, look, it's okay."

"You sure?"

"Sure I'm sure."

"Okay." She took the bucket from him. "Be back in a flash with the cash," she called leaping off into the darkness in a series of high, arching jetés. Kristina had no way of seeing the smile on Paul's face or how he lingered watching for her long after the darkness had shadowed her from sight.

"I can't believe this." Kristina looked down at the food on her plate. "I don't eat this fancy at home. You sure you'll have enough food left to last you, Paul?"

"Don't worry. I won't starve."

"But, biscuits—with jam no less. You're a couple of geniuses!" She had watched Jill and Paul construct a reflector oven from aluminum foil stretched over some wet sticks stuck into the sand close to the fire.

After gathering the stones they had put her to peeling the potatoes and carrots, which Jill cut into strips, buttered and salted, wrapped tightly in foil, and placed among the now hot coals of the fire. The carrots were not quite done, like Japanese vegetables, but the biscuits actually baked, even browned. The marinated meat they had cooked on a stick was the best of all.

"Your pack must have weighed a ton, Paul, to have all this stuff."

"It's very compact. Nothing big."

"How do you know so much about camping?"

"We've done it all my life. No big deal."

"We sure don't have much to contribute. Maybe some fruit . . . "

"And the s'mores," Jill interrupted.

"The what?"

"Here." Jill pulled out a candy bar, some marshmallows and graham crackers. "You roast the marshmallow until it's all hot and soft. Careful, don't let it catch fire, and then you put it between two crackers with a piece of chocolate candy. Presto, s'mores. Want to try one?"

Kristina snuggled down into the warmth of her sleeping bag. She was pleasantly tired and beginning to drowse off despite the hardness of the ground.

"He's nice." Jill's voice was quiet in the darkness.

"Who?"

"Paul."

"Oh. Sure."

"A great dancer."

"Uhm."

"He's stuck on you." Jill's comment brought Kristina back from the edge of sleep.

"Paul? You're crazy!"

"You're the crazy one. He can't take his eyes off you."

"Paul?" Jill's suggestion lay in Kristina's mind like a new toy. She examined it carefully, pushed it aside, and settled back to the business of sleep. "He's like a brother." She yawned.

"He doesn't think of you as his sister. Hey, let's get up early tomorrow and go swimming if it's still warm."

"Okay." And then she remembered. "I didn't bring my suit."

"Who needs a suit? We'll get up and go before anyone's on the beach."

"Swim naked?" The idea jerked Kristina fully awake.

"Why not?"

"I've never tried it before." She smiled toying with the idea. "I guess it's no big deal. They even have nude beaches."

"Yeah, but this isn't one. We'll have to be careful."

13

Kristina had no trouble waking early. Her back ached; her neck was stiff. "Oh," she groaned, "I think I've broken every bone in my body." She collapsed from her stretch. "Or at least bruised them all."

It was about five A.M. when the girls poked their heads out of the tent. The sun, although not up, warned of its coming with shafts of color outlining the horizon. The usual heavy dew was missing and already the air was warm. They grabbed their towels and headed for the beach, the sand cool between their toes.

The thought of bathing nude excited Kristina. All the way down to the water she searched apprehensively for signs of other early risers. "What if someone comes?" She continued looking behind them and up and down the beach.

"This time of morning? Only Indians and crazy people get up this early."

"Well, I guess I know where that puts me." Kristina laughed.

Jill dropped her towel on a pile of logs. The tide hadn't turned yet. It covered most of the beach. Kristina made the mistake of sticking her foot into a foamy wave that raced up to where they stood.

She gasped. "My God, it's freezing!"

"Stimulates the blood. Come on, you aren't going to chicken out are you?" Jill was already unzipping her jeans.

"Never." Kristina took one last look up and down the beach and threw her towel next to Jill's. She pulled her shirt over her head and reached around to untie her halter. Jill was already racing through the shallow waves, her bare bottom firm and white against the blackness of the water.

"Wait for me!" She stepped out of her underpants, kicked them carelessly toward the pile of clothes and towels, and raced after Jill. She was so anxious to hide herself in the water that it took a moment for the shock of the temperature to register.

"Wow!" she screeched. "It's pure ice!"

"Isn't it great? The only way to swim." Jill dove through a building breaker that crashed into Kristina knocking what breath was left from her lungs. She fought her way back to the surface. So far she had been so preoccupied that the pleasure of skinny dipping had eluded her. Her skin tingled as she struggled to breathe.

"I'm getting out. It's too cold," she called to Jill. She turned toward shore and her heart stopped. "Jill . . ." her voice was a whisper that only she could hear.

The two boys from yesterday stood guarding their clothes. The blond ponytailed one dangled a halter from his finger. Even from where she struggled to stand against the waves, Kristina recognized the sick grin on his face. "Jill . . ." Her voice rose hysterically. Jill swam over to her. "What are we going to do?" She tried to keep the fear from her voice, but she was almost rigid with it. The wave broke unheeded around the girls' shoulders.

"Careful," Jill soothed. "It's all right. Control yourself." Kristina felt the calm coolness of her friend's words. Of course, discipline, that's all she needed. Kristina was an expert on discipline. She tried to swallow the fear. *Control yourself.* She gritted her teeth, but there was no controlling the fear. Her heart, which had stopped on her discovery, now raced thumping in her throat. A huge breaker crashed knocking them over and for a moment the struggle took all Kristina's strength. It was as if she were back struggling with the tidal wave.

At last she stood, feet firmly on the sandy bottom, coughing and spitting salt water. By now her entire body was numb and she found it difficult to focus. Jill reached for her hand.

"It's all right, Kristy."

"How's the water, girls? Better not stay in too long. You'll catch cold," he taunted. Kristina remembered his eyes on her and felt an even deeper chill shudder through her.

"He's right. We can't stay in here much longer."

"I can't get out," Kristina whispered. "Not with them there. I'd rather die."

"That might just happen if we don't get out of here soon. The water's too cold. We can go into shock or hypothermia."

"I can't. . . ." She bit at her lower lip holding back the tears that threatened.

"Come on, Kristy." Jill pulled gently on her hand.

"But what'll we do? They have our clothes. They aren't just going to hand them over to us." Another wave washed over them. They struggled to stand against its force. By the time Kristina had wiped the water and sand from her eyes, she became aware of still another figure on the beach. The tears began to run down her cheeks in spite of all her efforts to blink them back. And then Jill's voice raised in jubilation.

"It's going to be okay. It's Paul! He'll help us." The two of them huddled together watching. The three figures stood poised, silhouetted against the early morning sunlight. Paul was taller than the others. It all started like the scene from *West Side Story* with Paul and the blond circling warily.

Kristina, almost numb with the cold, now felt a hot flash of fear. It would not be a fair fight. Paul didn't have a chance. What if they had knives?

Paul grabbed for the halter the boy was flouting, and then, as if caught up in slow motion, the two boys were locked together wrestling, first standing and then tripping and falling to the ground. They rolled over and over. The girls couldn't tell who was winning until the fourth figure stepped in grabbing Paul.

Kristina and Jill shivering, huddled close as they watched the park ranger frisk the three boys for weapons. The shouting, the fear, the pain of the fight was already becoming a dim echo on the receding breakers. Kristina didn't remember how or when, but both she and Jill were dressed in their shorts and halters. She gathered the beach towel about her, pulling it close.

"All right, you kids, just what's this ruckus all about?" But even as he asked he turned and glared at the girls. "As if I didn't know," he muttered.

"We weren't doing anything wrong," Jill retorted throwing her wet, bedraggled hair back from her face. "We were just swimming."

"Well, nude bathing is against the law here, young lady. The two of you are coming in with these rowdies."

"Paul was just trying to help," Kristina volunteered. But the man, impatient with the entire scene, was not about to listen.

"At least it's warm here." Kristina sat on the edge of a cot taking in the drab walls, the chainlink screen at the window, and the single sink.

"Sure. It's cozy. Hang a chief rug on the wall and it could be home." Jill's sarcasm framed Kristina's mood. What was her father going to say? She'd had to call him. The officials insisted. Besides, she didn't have the money to pay her fine.

Paul and the two girls waited outside in the hallway while their parents talked to the officer in charge. Kristina couldn't bring herself to look at him. She blanched remembering the fight. His eye was already black and blue, and there was a big lump on the side of his jaw. She wanted to say something to him. To thank him. The words just wouldn't come.

It was Jill who broke the silence. "Wow! Is that a beaut!" She reached up and touched Paul's eye. He flinched slightly. "If I had a raw steak, I'd offer it to you."

"If you did, I'd eat it." Paul laughed rubbing his stomach. "I'm not so sure I like starting the day with no breakfast. "He smiled shyly at Kristina. She returned his smile, hesitantly at first and then broadly. His grin widened crinkling around the corners of his eyes in the way she'd noticed before. Something stirred in her and she was blushing again, a blush that had nothing to do with the way he'd last seen her. The blush widened into a strange warm feeling that surged through her. She looked away. Just then the door opened and they were being ushered into the room.

It was two very subdued young girls who stood between Kristina's father and Jill's mother waiting to be officially released. "The law reads . . ." and the man behind the desk read in a dull tone from a thick blue book. The air was still, heavy, except for the furious sound of a fly against the window, and the scratching of pens edged by the ripping sounds of checks as both parents paid the fine. No one said a word.

Kristina's father was silent. The sound of the tires on the pavement filled the car. They had stopped at the camp to gather her things and say good-bye to Jill. The weather remained hot, filling the beach with eager sun worshipers and leaving Kristina wistful that she could not stay.

She sneaked a glance now and then at her father's profile.

The jaw was firm, almost protruding. He stared straight ahead looking neither left nor right, except when his driving required it. The hum of the tires accentuated the silence. She wished she could turn on the radio to fill the car with some sort of noise, but she held her hands in her lap and continued to stare straight ahead. Finally she blurted out, "I didn't lie . . . not really. You asked who was taking us. Well, Jill's mother did take us."

He turned his head and looked at her then looked at the highway.

"Oh, all right. I knew what you meant, but I was afraid you wouldn't let me go. Would you?"

The question hung unanswered for what seemed like forever to Kristina. "Yes." He spoke the word quietly, not looking at her.

"You would?" Her disbelief echoed.

"You're sixteen, Kristina. It's time you tried your wings."

"I know, but . . ." She looked at him still not believing. "You really would have let me go?" The muscles along his jaw didn't seem so thick now and she could have sworn she saw his lips twitch in what looked like a smile.

"How was it?"

His question didn't register. "W-what?" she stuttered.

"The skinny-dipping. How was it?"

She looked at him, her mouth open. "I—I—I don't know." She gulped. "I mean I don't remember. The water was so cold, and I was so scared somebody would come." There was no doubt about it, he was smiling.

"That must have been one hell of a ruckus!" He turned and grinned at her. "Wish I could have seen it."

Kristina's mouth dropped and then a warm feeling rushed through her. She continued to stare at him. He really wasn't ticked at all. Suddenly she wanted to share it all. "You can't imagine how scared I was when I saw them there. My mind just went blank. Those boys were so gross, especially the one with the long dirty hair. He gave me the chills the way he looked at me. I mean I felt naked even when I had clothes on. I don't know what I'd have done if Jill and Paul hadn't been there. He took them both on. He didn't have a chance."

"That surprised me."

"What?"

"Paul. I guess you ballet dancers are tougher than I gave you credit for." He winked at her.

She could hardly contain the warmth. It flooded through her and spilled over into a wide grin. Eagerly she began telling her father all about Jill and the neat dinner Paul and she had cooked the night before. "It's really great there, Daddy." The word felt strange on her lips. How long had it been since she had called him that? For years it had been father. She hesitated then plunged on, "Camping is fantastic. There's so much to learn. Paul knew how to do everything. Jill too. Can we go camping sometime? It's so beautiful. We could buy a tent and some sleeping bags and—"

"I don't know. I suppose Anna might be . . ."

It all vanished. All the warmth and closeness drained from her like water from a leaky pail. What was she thinking of? Of course, they couldn't go camping with Anna. For a moment Kristina had forgotten. It was gone. The companionship she had felt just a moment ago. Had she imagined it? They drove on in silence.

14

He wasn't for the idea. She could tell. "I don't see any point to it, Kristina. What do you expect him to accomplish? We've had all the finest doctors for your mother. It's not an evil spell you know, something a medicine man can dance away. Her spinal cord was smashed."

Although she made no motion, it was as if Kristina had put her hands over her ears. She would not listen. She watched him curiously—his mouth, his eyes, his hands. He stopped, waiting expectantly. She came back with a start. "Ah, well, he's interesting, Daddy." (The name had now become familiar. Only when she became annoyed with him did she revert back to father.) "He knows a lot about plants and you know how Anna loves plants. He uses them for healing, for making secret potions."

"To do what?"

"Oh, I don't know. They know how to dig up soap and stun fish so you can scoop them out. Please, Daddy. I'm not even sure he'll come, but it would be good for her. I know."

He paused waiting for her to go on. When she didn't, he shrugged. "It might be good for her at that, but what about you? Just as long as you aren't expecting any great miracle."

"Oh, thank you, Daddy. I can't wait to ask Jill." She turned and started for the door.

"Kristina..." There was an urgency in his voice. She stopped and turned back to him.

"Yes?"

"Remember what I said about miracles, kitten."

She was nervous. The idea of Jill's grandfather was exciting, but now that she was actually going to meet him. What do you say to an Indian medicine man? She came down the school steps with Jill and there he was, driving a car. She didn't know why, but it seemed all wrong. Medicine men didn't drive cars. They rode horses bareback, and he looked out of place behind the wheel of Jill's station wagon.

He wore his hair, which had been very dark but was now a mixture of gray, pulled back and tied with a piece of rawhide. His face was weathered, the wrinkles folding one into the other, mapping out the years in copper etchings. He was a very small man, hardly able to see over the steering wheel. Kristina's heart dropped. She didn't know what she had expected but certainly not this small wrinkled man in a blue-plaid flannel shirt. Her images of a powerful, soul-stirring, mind-healing man vanished.

Jill slid into the front seat. "Grandfather." She leaned over and kissed him on the cheek. Kristina wondered if he even felt the softness of her lips through his leathery skin. "I want you to meet Kristy." She motioned to her. Kristina slid into the front seat next to Jill. "Kristy, this is my grandfather, Pioto."

"Hello, sir." She didn't know if she should offer to shake hands. Finally she did nothing but smile thinly.

"Hello, Kristina."

His voice was ordinary, too, like any nice old man, any grandfather. Not a mysterious, powerful medicine man. She swallowed at the disappointment that caught in her throat.

His eyes lingered on her face. They were a funny color.

Like Jill's. Speckled trout. She wanted to look away but found she couldn't. It had never happened to her before. No one had ever got inside her. She felt him probing the small crevices hidden away within her mind and she wanted to run. It frightened her and yet excited her. Kristina was mesmerized by Pioto. She caught her breath. Why had she thought he was a little man? She became aware that both of them were staring at her waiting for an answer to some question she had not heard.

"W-what?" she stuttered, "I—"

"Grandfather wanted to know about your mother."

"Anna?"

"Why do you call her that?"

"That's her name."

"Have you always called your mother by her first name?"

"Well . . . I . . ." Kristina paused peeling back layers of her memory trying to recall. "She's always been Annya."

"You said her name was Anna." He would not let her look away.

"Annya was my pet name for her. When I was little, Anna came out Annya."

"You don't call her Annya anymore?"

She licked her lips nervously. She wanted to leave it be, but he waited, eyes probing. Resentment formed in a tight little ball. Some things were personal, private. Only with her mother had she felt comfortable in sharing those things. She looked upon others as intruders. Even her father. "No, I guess I call her Anna now." She turned away and looked out the window.

He would not let her run. "Tell me about her injuries."

Kristina fidgeted. She hated to repeat the doctor's diagnosis. If you said it, it was true. Final. She avoided remembering their pronouncements, their odds predicting percentages like crap-game jockeys. She briefly outlined her mother's condition.

Pioto studied her deliberately. It was almost as if he were more interested in her reaction to Anna, than in Anna's condition. Again she turned from him and stared out the window trying to shake the uneasiness that gripped her. He said nothing more, started the car, and drove silently toward Kristina's house.

Martha met them at the door, her usual smile of greeting missing. Instead she was about as friendly as a snapping turtle. Hands on hips, she stood, feet planted firmly blocking the entrance.

"Martha!" She didn't budge. Kristina pushed past the hostile woman forcing her back into the hall. "This is my friend Jill and her grandfather, Pioto." She waited for Martha's acknowledgement. Finally, the woman grunted and half-nodded at Jill and then fastened her eyes on Pioto. Kristina could see her looking down her nose, measuring the old Indian. Her eyes locked on the small bag he carried. It was the same one Jill had shared with her earlier.

"And what might that be?" Martha pointed at Pioto indicating the bag with such distaste that Kristina had to look again to make sure it was the same bag she remembered.

"Martha!" The woman turned reluctantly. "I think we'd like a cup of tea. I'll take Jill and Pioto to meet Anna. Is Daddy home?"

"No. He was called out. But he expects to be coming back any minute now. Maybe you should be waiting."

"You know how unpredictable Daddy is. I'm sure he would want me to introduce our guests to Anna."

Martha moved toward the kitchen muttering, eyeing Pioto. "Never did trust Injuns!" Although the words were muttered under her breath, they were quite audible. Kristina couldn't believe her ears. She'd never seen Martha act this way. She looked quickly at Jill and Pioto to see if they had heard. Neither looked perturbed.

"I don't know what's got into that woman." She ushered

the two of them down the hall toward the back study and Anna. When they entered the room, Anna was in her usual position, back to the door, facing the ocean. She didn't turn upon their entrance. Maybe she was asleep. Kristina moved around in front of her mother. Anna's attention shifted slowly from the sea to the girl in front of her. It was as if she were a stranger and then slowly Kristina saw recognition awaken in Anna's eyes. The past few weeks she had become aware of her mother's continued withdrawal. There was less and less communication now, a wall of silence building between them. Brick by brick. Higher and higher. Sometimes laid by Anna, sometimes by Kristina. Kristina could see it happening with relentless finality. Even though she wanted to stop it, wanted to tear at the wall to bring back the laughter, the love, something was working against her and Anna. Something inside the both of them.

"Anna, you have company." Slowly Anna turned to face her guests. "This is my friend Jill, who I told you about, and her grandfather, Pioto." She watched her mother, waiting.

"Hello." Anna's voice was distant but polite. Her eyes flicked over Jill and Pioto casually and then resettled on Pioto. Interest flashed across her face. Her body tensed beneath his gaze. She leaned forward. Kristina held her breath. A strange electric silence settled over the room as the two of them, Anna and Pioto, continued to gaze at each other. Kristina felt dizzy and then realized she was holding her breath. The harsh sound of it escaping went unnoticed as Anna and Pioto continued to communicate in a silent way.

Jill and Kristina might not even have been there. Pioto sank to the floor in a smooth effortless motion of a younger man and sat quietly in front of Anna.

"We'd better go." Jill's voice, although only a whisper, startled her. They turned and moved from the room closing the door softly. Kristina leaned against it. She couldn't help the thumping of her heart. There was no doubt Pioto had touched something in Anna. She wanted to reach out and hug Jill. Instead she grinned impishly, grabbed her friend's hand, and pulled her along the hall.

"Come on. Come see my room. It's the neatest room in the whole wide world!" She ran ahead taking the stairs two at a time, leaped into the air, spun about gracefully, opened her door, and showed Jill through.

Jill stopped just inside. A low whistle echoed across the room. "You're right." The windows on the ocean side soared from floor to ceiling creating a living mural. The entire north wall was mirrored behind her exercise bar so that she could study her reflection correcting, improving her position and movements. The floor was a deep, rich parquet that glowed warm with shadows like a forest on a sunny day. Her bed was an old-fashioned walnut sleigh bed that she and Anna had found on one of their foraging trips through junk stores and antique shops.

The very best though was the loft that her father had created. A place to hide. To dream. To run. It was edged with a wooden railing and a handcrafted ladder for Kristina to climb. It was her dream world. Like a tree house, it was a special place that held her most precious treasures: her sand dollar collection, beach agates, a Japanese float she'd found after a big Southwestern storm. They were all stored safely in a handcarved box from India that Anna had brought her. "A magic box, Kristy, that hides all the ancient mysteries of gurus, maharajas within it." They'd laughed over the possibilities.

Jill walked quietly about the room touching the warm wood paneling, scuffing her feet through the soft lamb rug. She stopped and stared through the windows at the wide expanse of the sea. Kristina stood silently beside her, her own pleasure rekindled. Jill turned slowly and studied the loft for a long moment and then walked over to the hand-made ladder running her hand tenderly over its smooth, warm finish. "I've never seen anything like it. Can I go up?"

"Sure. Come on." Kristina led the way. She settled herself on a large pillow and tossed one to Jill as she stuck her head up over the top.

"Want to see my India box?"

They settled themselves on the cushions and she opened the large handcarved box. She fingered each item tenderly, hesitantly. Where she had been eager to share, she now became uncertain. What if Jill thought her treasures silly? Worthless? She removed each item carefully examining it before offering it to her friend.

First came the beach treasures. The three perfect sand dollars with their poinsettia design, each rattling its mystic secret, the abalone shell with its mother of pearl iridescence, the large pink conch. Kristina put it up to her ear reassuring herself of its continued whisperings before handing it to Jill.

She hesitated, waiting to see her friend's reaction. Jill touched each piece, carefully running her fingers over the design and shape, shaking them gently, even smelling them. Kristina relaxed with a sigh for she recognized the pleasure on her friend's face and her apprehension fled.

Kristina fingered the smooth piece of driftwood shaped like a flying bird and then passed it on. She offered no explanation, told no tales of discoveries. It was a silent sharing until she got down near the bottom of the box. When she pulled out a small pair of very worn ballet slippers, she tied the ribbon laces gently. "My first toe slippers." She hesitated until Jill held out her hand and then she passed them on. The very last thing she took from the box was a small piece of white tissue paper. She held it for a moment before opening it. She stared down at its contents so long that finally even Jill became impatient and leaned over to see what she was looking at. Curled tightly against the white of the paper were three dark rusty curls of hair too dark to be her own. For a moment Kristina was oblivious of her friend, of time, of . . . the shrill wail brought her back.

"My God!" Both girls flinched as if they had been struck. The wailing continued fluctuating from a moan to a high screech. Kristina pushed the box aside, scrambled up from her pillow, and clambered down the ladder with Jill following on her heels. They rushed down the hall toward the sound coming from Anna's room. Kristina burst through the door and stopped dead. Martha, wild-eyed, broom in hand, was circling Pioto waving it up and down shrieking in a sing-song fashion. Like a primeval sorceress, she seemed to be battling some unseen power. Pioto stood, unblinking, holding a pipe that smelled pungent, like burning sage. Both Anna and Pioto appeared to be hypnotized watching Martha as she circled about them.

"What on earth . . . Martha!" Kristina's voice rang through the room, but the woman continued her strange wailing and sweeping motion. "Martha!" This time it was a shout. The woman hesitated and Kristina moved forward, took the broom from her, turned her bodily toward the door, and half-pushed her from the room.

"I'm sorry." Kristina wrung her hands nervously. Pioto sat behind the wheel, Jill next to him. "I don't know what got into her. She must have, well I don't know, maybe she's been drinking. This certainly has never happened before. Usually Martha's so . . . "

It was Jill that came to Kristina's rescue. "It's okay, Kristy. Don't worry about it."

"But . . . "

Pioto turned and looked at her. She stopped her stammering. His eyes held hers. Her heart stopped. "Anna?"

"They are right. Your mother will never walk." The words

struck at a corner of Kristina that she had held in reserve. A tiny little niche of hope that she had not exposed, even to herself.

She stood watching as the car pulled out of the drive into the road. Jill was waving, but Kristina didn't lift her hand to respond. She turned and made her way up the stairs. Carefully she closed the door behind her. She shut her eyes and leaned heavily against it trying to blot out Pioto's face and words.

"I'm sorry, missy." She looked up at Martha who stood in the hall. The woman was gripping the broom handle until her knuckles showed white. Her eyes were shiny with unshed tears. "I don't know what got into me. It must have been his chanting and that awful smell. I guess I went a wee bit crazy. I mean I thought he was trying to harm the missus, trying to put an evil spell on her."

"It's all right, Martha." Her voice was very tired. She pushed herself away from the door. "It doesn't matter."

15

"Why don't you come over? We'll go down to the beach or up in the hills." Jill leaned against the locker watching Kristina fuss.

"I can't."

"Why not?"

"I gotta go downtown."

Jill waited, but Kristina didn't explain. "What do you do every Tuesday rushing off so mysteriously? You got a secret lover?"

"Don't be silly. I gotta go. I'll miss my bus." Kristina kicked the locker door shut and turned away from Jill. "See you tomorrow."

She didn't know why she didn't tell Jill about her Tuesdays in the hospital. What was the big deal? She went to learn to help Anna. That's what she told herself, but that didn't explain it all. The thrill of being near David Feldman—Dr. David as she'd come to call him—or the disappointment she felt when he didn't appear. How she snapped at Martha and her father on those days.

Of course he didn't know how he affected her. She acted very aloof. Cool. But when he patted her cheek or touched her arm, she was sure he could see how wildly her heart was beating.

"What do you suppose my story is today?" Kristina sat on the floor, the children close beside her.

"The Cat in the Hat!" one of them shouted.

"Oh, you guessed. How did you know?"

"Your hat," they squealed and pointed to Kristina's hat.

"Do you like it?" She held her head very still balancing the wicker basket topped with an old whisk broom. The dish rags and tin cans dangled about her ears.

"Yeah!" They clapped their hands.

The day had gone well. When Kristina could escape into the stories she told, she forgot her pity. She didn't have to swallow the tears that lay just behind her eyes, or fake enthusiasm for tiny accomplishments like eight-year-old Sarah buttoning her dress or six-year-old Jimmy fitting pegs into holes.

All those feelings came rushing, overwhelming her at the oddest times like when Allison's mother came for her. The pain in her eyes. Watching someone's hopes and dreams gradually fade was almost more than Kristina could stand. But she hid it well. Her voice boomed, filled with laughter. Hope like David? Well, no, but she did his other big thing. Kristina worked like hell.

When Ruth, the nurse, asked her to dance for the children, Kristina became excited and eager. What should she dance? There was the scene with Peter Pan and Captain Hook, or something from *Sleeping Beauty*. No, she wanted it to be light and happy. Finally she chose the "Dance of the Sugar-Plum Fairy" from the *Nutcracker Suite* and for the first time in a long while, she went eagerly to her practice bar.

Kristina loved her costume. It was so white and frilly like sugar crystals. Her hair, intertwined through the sparkling tiara, was piled loosely on top of her head. Her white toe slippers were laced tightly about her legs. She peeked in on the children who sat rigidly in straight rows. Their eagerness was apparent in the way they gripped each other's hands trying to still themselves. She shared their excitement, was filled with the same tight anticipation that she felt on opening night of a new performance.

The nurses from the floor had joined the children and were sitting on the floor with them waiting for her. Kristina poised herself. Ruth turned on the record and she entered lightly, the way fairies do. A hushed sigh rushed through the children and the magic fell like star dust from her wand. Caught up in her world of music and rhythm, she did not dance the part but became the Sugar Plum Fairy. A mystical journey from one world to another. She loved her world of toy soldiers, china dolls, toy drums, and dancing clowns. As always, the faces of her audience blurred and she became one with the music.

From a slow, beautiful arabesque she moved through a startling routine of plié, jetés, and battements. The elevations were pure joy for her. She could not imagine ever enjoying ballet being confined to the ground the way the early ballerinas were. Her legs flashed, dipped, and leaped carrying her beyond the room of crippled children; forgetting momentarily her mother; leaving behind the misunderstandings between her and her father; even the peculiar heart fluttering caused by David. She was in her own world now, the one she understood with every part of her being. The children all became caught up in her magic... all but one.

If every eye had not been so intent upon Kristina, someone would have noticed the change of expression on Allison's face. Her usual look of disinterest changed gradually to despair and then to something hard to describe. Envy? No, something even stronger. It was an emotion so strong that it cut through the strength and beauty of Tchaikovsky and caught at the dancing girl. In mid-air the jeté that started so perfectly with strength and grace seemed to meet an unseen obstacle wilting in its perfection into something unfamiliar. Kristina became confused. Suddenly she was back, aware of the children and finally of Allison. Where her movements had been strong and fluid, they became tentative, almost hesitant. What could have happened? Where had the magic gone?

Kristina's eagerness to share her talent had been so pure, so free of any of her other emotions, but it became clouded. What was it she felt? Guilt! It hit her as if someone had slapped her hard. She almost stumbled on a simple jeté. Allison hated her because of her legs, her perfect control of the tiniest movement. In her confusion she forgot where she was and stopped still. Even the children who had never seen the ballet before knew something was wrong. A rustling of question murmured through the room. Kristina tried to recapture the spirit, but it was gone. Finally she performed the coda as best she could and turned and fled the room.

Ruth followed her. "What happened, Kristina? What is the matter?"

"Didn't you see the look on her face?" Her voice was a small whisper. "Allison. She hates me. She . . ." Kristina ran from the room, down the hall to the lounge.

"It wasn't you she hated." David leaned close to Kristina, who was curled up in the corner of the bit leather couch. Her tiara had slipped sideways; her hair spilled down covering half of her face. She brushed at it with a careless hand.

"Did you know she was studying gymnastics? Her mother had enrolled her at Perkins when she was four. In less than a year she had become one of its most promising students. Allison loved it. Spent at least an hour a day on the balance beam. It isn't you she hates."

"I've never felt anything like that before. It was so strong that it reached out and broke into my mind even while I danced."

David was silent for a long while then he took her hand and held it warmly. 'You're a very brave girl, Kristina." He patted her hand absently. "And you are doing a great job with the children, but you haven't managed to overcome it yet have you?"

Kristina tossed her head back clearing the hair from her face. "What?"

"The guilt."

"What guilt?"

"The guilt you feel about not being crippled."

"But . . . " Kristina started to protest.

"No. Now tell me what is the first thing you feel when you see Allison or Jimmy or Sarah? Pity. Right?" He didn't wait for her to answer but went on. "Pity builds walls. It prevents relationships and most of all acceptance for what you are and what you can be. Pity robs people of goals and achievements, but worst of all, it robs them of self-respect."

Kristina lowered her head. She tried to blink back the tears, but they slid silently down her cheeks. "What can I do?"

He had to lean close to her to hear her words. "It's a special talent, Kristina. Not everyone can do it. It takes courage. I'm proud of you for wanting to try but . . . "

She shook her head vigorously. "No. You don't understand. I *must* learn."

16

Kristina couldn't forget the incident with Allison or David's words. She mulled them over and over and finally out of the need to talk to someone, she confided in Jill about her visits to the hospital. She didn't mention David. It was the episode with Allison, her confusion, "And after all that you know what Ruth suggested I do? Teach those kids ballet! Isn't that the most ridiculous thing you've ever heard?" She paused waiting for Jill to agree with her.

"I don't know. Maybe it's not so ridiculous after all."

"You crazy? How could I possibly teach those..." she paused, searching, "handicapped children ballet?" Kristina looked at Jill as if she had just suggested she teach fish to fly. Jill didn't respond to her outburst, but stared at her in that probing way that made Kristina uncomfortable.

"They have hands don't they? They can move, maybe not perfectly like you. You are very good with all your leaps. You fly, but there is the other part. Are you aware of the subtle movements of the head? The hands? Even the way you point your toes?"

"No!" Kristina almost shouted the word. The very thought of anyone doing the dance who couldn't fly was blasphemous. She stopped midstride in her agitated pacing and stared defiantly at Jill.

Jill did not back down, but stared back unblinking. "Why not?"

"*Why not?*" "*Why not?*" The question echoed inside Kristina's head. "*Why not?*" The question clung to her mind like an unwanted burr. "I m-mean—" she stuttered and resumed her pacing. "Well, you know. They aren't coordinated enough to . . . how can you expect them to . . ."

"That's it isn't it? Expecting them to be like you."

"Well no!" Kristina turned red. "It's not that."

"Isn't it? You know perfection is your hang-up not theirs. You don't have to be an eagle to fly. What about penguins? Now there's a bird that doesn't know a thing about flying. You're right. They'll never dance like you—"

"No!" She tried to pluck it out, but the idea stuck, unwanted. "I couldn't." Kristina shuddered remembering Allison's look.

"Why?" Jill was like a broken record that wouldn't stop.

Kristina rolled the question around in her mind examining it. She remembered the excitement of the other children, how the music had charmed them, had let them escape.

"Why? It's impossible that's all." She turned away from Jill. "I gotta go." She left her friend without looking back. Instead of going home along the path through the hills as she usually did, Kristina cut across the road and down to the beach.

The late spring fog rolled in just above the water wrapping itself around her legs like a friendly kitten. She welcomed its solitude as it rose to envelope her. She walked along the water's edge oblivious of the sporadic wailing of the fog horn. She scrambled up the sand now and then to escape the waves, then paused, removed her sandals, and continued along the foam-whipped edge. The sound of the surf was muffled by the thick gray blanket that shrouded her magnifying the sounds of her own thoughts. Jill's words echoed over and over. *"Perfection is your hang-up." "Perfection."* Then David's words joined. *"Accept." "Accept."*

What kind of person was she anyway? Even Allison could see through her. Kristina had thought she was hiding her feelings so well, but it was not only the dance incident. Allison had caught her unaware before. She had been standing over Billy's crib. For a moment she had forgotten to mask her pity and it was there for all to see. How could he not be the perfect child that he looked? How could anyone accept the fact that he'd grow into an awkward boy. The tragedy. She could not hide the pity that swept through her. She looked up to catch Allison watching her. She tried to smile to hide the revulsion she had felt, but it was too late. Allison's look was so piercing, so knowing that she had to turn away from it. And now this. The dancing. Jill saying she could teach them. Ridiculous! The knot inside Kristina tightened. Why did she feel so angry at the thought of those poor little things trying to learn ballet. Any part of it? The very thought seemed ludicrous. Kristina kicked at the water that had numbed her ankles. The idea clung stubbornly.

She let herself into the house quietly. It was silent except for the soft sounds of music coming from Anna's retreat. Kristina glanced at her watch. Dinner wasn't for another hour. She should probably ask Martha if she needed any help, but instead she slipped up the stairs to her room. Without thinking she threw her books and sandals on the bed and walked over to her exercise bar. Whenever she had a problem, she went to her bar. Her mind seemed to work better. She began the simple warm-up routine and then stopped. The sand that clung to her toes and heels made her uncomfortable. She rubbed the bottom of her feet against first one leg and then the other and started again. She stopped again irritated by the fine, almost invisible, grains. She looked around and made her way to the lambskin rug next to her bed. She walked through it scuffing her feet in the soft fur. As she turned to return to her bar she stopped, studying the pile of records. Maybe she'd work out to some music. As she thumbed through the pile absently there was a knock on the door.

Her father found her surrounded by stacks of records. "What's up, Kristina? Martha could use a little help."

"In a minute, Daddy, I'm looking for a record."

"It looks like you have a few."

"I mean one of my dance records. One that..." She paused and looked up at her father. She studied him for a long moment as if considering a possibility. "Do you suppose..." Then rejecting the idea she rose from the rug leaving the records. "It's ridiculous. Jill's crazy!" She moved toward the door.

"Can I get into this argument, or is it a one-person battle?"

She paused. She was very close to him, so close she became aware of the small gray flecks in his blue eyes, the creases that she hadn't noticed before etching lines like fine webs not only from around his eyes but also his mouth. His sideburns were long showing the dark red color that his beard would be if he let it grow. He looked older, more tired than she'd ever seen him. "Daddy..." Suddenly Kristina wished she were a little girl. She wanted him to hold her and cuddle her. To rock her. She longed to reach out to him, but she never had. She didn't know how. "I guess it's kind of a one-man battle. You see, Jill thinks I can teach those children ballet. Isn't that ridiculous?" She paused waiting for him to agree with her, wanting him to.

"Well..." She could see him turning the idea over examining it in his methodical way and all of a sudden she was angry.

"Of course it is!" She shouted and turned, rushing past him out the door into the hall.

17

Maybe it was the fog, the dampness that clung to everything, the wailing of the foghorn, that depressed Kristina. She walked along the street dragging her feet. It was Tuesday. She didn't want to go to the hospital. Even the prospect of seeing David didn't perk her up. He'd been so busy last week that he'd hardly even spoken to her. She moved along slowly staring into the drab shop windows not really seeing the wares on display until it caught her eye.

She stopped, pressing close to the gray oil-smeared glass of the antique store. Was it? She cupped her hands shielding her eyes trying to focus on the object that lay in a tray of old buttons. Her breath caught. It was. She turned from the window and made her way through the door that clanged her entrance.

She cradled the stone in her palm. It was bigger than Jill's and shaped like a crescent. The shop was poorly lit, but still the stone glowed faintly like fog when the sun's rays penetrate its moisture.

"It's a moonstone, isn't it?" She looked up at the proprietor. Not the usual old person one would expect in the dusty shop, but a dark, intense, almost sinister looking, man.

He reached out taking the stone from her, examined it carefully and then rubbed it on his shirt sleeve. He looked at her thoughtfully as he continued to polish it.

"What do you know about the moonstone?"

"Uh . . . not much. Just what my friend told me."

"And what was that?"

"Oh, just that the Indians thought it had special powers."

"To do what?"

"Well . . . " Kristina hesitated, "Oh it's just an old Indian legend."

"That you place it with the dying person to insure a safe journey to the next world?"

"You've heard it too?" Kristina couldn't hide the surprise in her voice.

"Yes, I've heard it." He stopped polishing and let the stone lay quietly in his open palm.

"Can I buy it?" She held her breath waiting for his answer.

"What for?" His eyes probed. Kristina flinched at their intensity.

"I'd just like to have it." He continued to stare at her, then shrugged.

"For five dollars you can have it or anything else in the place."

Kristina walked out into the fog her heart thumping, the moonstone wrapped safely in her purse. Why had she bought it? Just what exactly was she going to do with it? She shivered at the possibilities the way she had when Jill was telling her of the potion Pioto made from big root.

The wall between Anna and her was growing higher each day, but a moment didn't pass that Kristina didn't feel her despair and long to help her. What was the feeling she had? What did it have to do with the moonstone?

The fog had thickened into a velvet cloak. As she moved along the street toward the hospital the thought of the moonstone caught up inside her making her heart beat erratically, forcing her to gulp at the heavy air to fill lungs that felt too large for her breast. She paused attempting to quiet the static within her. Absently she looked through the café window.

At first his face didn't register because he was turned slightly away from her and her mind was filled with the moonstone. It was a vague prodding that made her squint for a closer look at the man that sat across from the lovely, young woman with heavy, dark hair. He reached out and took her hand in an intimate gesture and Kristina gasped. All thoughts of the moonstone drained from her. She couldn't believe her eyes. Surely . . . she reached up as if to push away the gauze of fog that lay between her and the window. There was no mistake. Her father smiled and leaned toward the woman. He looked young, younger then he had since . . .

Kristina whirled away from the window and stumbled down the street. It couldn't be. He wouldn't. She turned away from the hospital. She couldn't face those poor crippled children or David or . . . she walked head down hands thrust deep into her pockets.

A numbness spread through Kristina. "So what?" she muttered. What did she expect? After all he's human and Anna . . . Anna would never be whole again. Rodney Lowrey was a young man. He had needs. Kristina tried to convince herself of the logic of the need, but she failed. She felt betrayed for Anna. How could he? She was so engulfed with her feelings that she didn't hear the car honk or see the red light or. . . . Strange . . . that last moment before the car hit her was like a movie slowed down with her becoming the observer not the participant. The squealing of brakes, the shouting. It all seemed so distant, so removed. The last thing she remembered before the pain exploded in her head was the look of horror on the driver's face.

It was very quiet and dark except for an intermittent buzzing of bells. Kristina struggled to place the sound. She opened her eyes and then closed them against the pain that throbbed against her skull. Gradually she became aware of deep breathing nearby. She turned her head carefully toward the sound and opened her eyes again. The small light near the head of the bed cast only smudges of light. She squinted at the large form sitting near the bed asleep in an uncomfortable position head rolled to one side. As she grew accustomed to the darkness Kristina recognized her father.

She studied him for a long time. Unguarded in sleep, his face looked . . . Kristina searched for the right word. Sorrowful. The fatigue lines etched around his mouth had deepened from the tiny creases she remembered to deep furrows. What was to become of them? How could she blame him for reaching out to a young, beautiful woman like the one in the café? He was young yet, still in his forties. She began to cry quietly.

She tried to turn away when a sharp pain jolted her. What was the matter? How badly was she hurt? What if, what if she was crippled! Kristina had to know. She flung back the sheet. Ignoring the pain that shot through her head and back, she swung her legs over the edge of the bed. Carefully she edged herself off placing her feet on the floor. Clinging to the bed, she stood tentatively. Relief swept through her. It was all right. She could stand. She let go, took one step and the pain swept through her with such force that she cried out and collapsed in an agonized heap.

"Kristina! Kristina!" Her father was bending over her.

"I'm crippled, Daddy! I'm crippled!" She clung to him clutching at him.

"No, kitten. It's okay. You're going to be okay." He held her close rocking her back and forth. "You're going to be fine." Gently he gathered her up and placed her back on the bed. He smoothed back her hair and brushed the tears from her cheeks. "You're just bruised, Kristina, and sore; but you're not crippled."

She clung to him even tighter absorbing his warmth, his strength. She needed him so badly.

"I'm sorry, Daddy." She buried her face against his chest. The two of them clung together in the darkness.

"Thank God you're okay." He pushed her away from him as if to see for himself and then drew her close again resting his chin on top her head. "You must not have been watching where you were going. You were lucky, though. The fog was so thick the car had slowed down to a crawl."

"I'm really okay? You're not just saying that?"

"It's just some nasty bruises and a slight concussion. David says you'll be out of here in no time."

"David?"

"Yes. He was on duty when they brought you in. I must say you picked a good spot to have an accident. They just brought you in on a stretcher." He was holding her hands and smiling at her in the dim light. Just like she'd seen him through the café window. Memory of them caught at her stiffening her. She wanted to ask him who she was. "Daddy?"

"Yes?"

She couldn't. The words stuck in her throat. She shivered slightly and withdrew her hands from his. "Oh, nothing." She turned away closing her eyes.

"You rest now, kitten. I'll stay right here with you."

"No." The word came out sharper than she had intended. She turned back. "I mean, it's silly for you to stay here with me and try to sleep in that awful chair. You should go home. Anna needs you."

"Well. Hello there you sleepyhead." Kristina opened her eyes. Sun streamed through the window. David stood near her bed looking down at her. He picked up her wrist and concentrated on his watch. "You gave us quite a scare, young lady. You always so careless about crossing streets?" He still held her hand although he was through taking her pulse. Warmth surged through her and she smiled.

"I'm all right?"

"All except for some fantastic bruises which will decorate your anatomy for a while and a royal headache for a day or two."

"How long will I have to stay?"

"Now what's the matter? Don't like our accomodations? Here you've just arrived and already . . . "

"You know what I mean."

"A day or two so we can check you out and then you can get back to your jetés and pliés or whatever." He covered her hand with his other one and studied her quietly. He became very serious. "You're a beautiful girl, Kristina, and a very, very lucky one." He patted her hand, turned and left.

She thought she was going to burst with the happiness that flooded through her. He liked her. She could see it in his eyes. He really liked her. She smiled and hugged herself barely wincing at the pain that her movement caused.

18

They came together. Paul, lean and lanky, and Jill. Kristina was still at a loss to categorize Jill. She was pretty and homely. She was tolerant and intolerant. She was proud and yet that was one thing she was sure of. In many ways Jill was the most humble person she had ever met. One minute Kristina thought she knew Jill and then snap—just like that—Jill would do something so totally unexpected, so unpredictable. Kristina was never sure.

She lay in her bed her hair piled loosely on top her head (it made her look older that way). Her favorite emerald robe which her father had brought was wrapped loosely about her. Kristina smiled at her friends.

"If it isn't the reigning queen. You sure you didn't do all this intentionally just to get a lot of attention?"

"Oh, Jill." Kristina grinned and then groaned clutching her side. "You should see the bruises. I'm like a spinach and egg salad, all yellow and green. Hi, Paul. How's Mr. Fellini? I can just see him having tantrums at my inconsiderateness. Who's taking my part?"

"Take your part?" He moved toward the bed and continued dramatically. "Who in the whole wide world could possibly . . ." Kristina smiled, not at the silliness of his words but at the picture he made: thin to the point of skinny, Adam's apple twitching spastically, nervous switching of his tissue-wrapped rose from one hand to the other. She waited expectantly, smiling, but his eyes were glued to the wall just above her head. He continued shifting the rose from side to side while he cleared his throat.

"Are you okay? You'll still be able to dance? I mean . . ."

"Why don't you give her the rose, Paul?" Jill's voice was warm, amused.

"Oh, sure. Here." He handed the flower to her.

"Thank you. It's beautiful." She dipped her head to inhale its spicy fragrance. Just then David came into the room. Kristina's eyes brightened.

"David, I mean Dr. Feldman, I want you to meet my friends Jill Hangtree and Paul Rolland."

"Hello." David smiled nodding at her visitors then he turned back to Kristina, who continued to sniff at the rose twisting it slightly. She hoped he noticed her hair and the way the robe set off the light tan she had managed to acquire. "Well, I'd say you were making the most of this—flowers, friends." He continued to smile at her. "And why not? One doesn't run down a car every day! How do you feel, young lady?"

"Truthfully, doctor, I have this . . ." and Kristina made a sweeping motion with her arm. She winced and then smiled broadly trying to cover up, "dismal pain in the upper cranium."

"Humph! I'll be back later. Don't believe a word she utters. She's delirious!" He waved at Paul and Jill and left. Kristina watched him move away, stop to say something to a nurse causing her to grin broadly, and then he disappeared through the door. Her smile faded visibly and her eyes dimmed. She continued to stare into the emptiness he had left behind.

"Wow!" Jill whistled. "Who was that?"

Kristina continued to stare. Jill leaned forward and

snapped her fingers beneath her nose. She jumped. "W-what . . . I'm sorry." She turned back to Paul and Jill.

"Just who was that?"

"David? I mean Dr. Feldman?"

"Yeah, Dr. Feldman. I mean how long has he been listening to your heartbeat with his stethoscope?"

"He's not really my doctor. I mean he specializes in children."

"Well . . . "

"I'm no child!" Kristina snapped at Jill, but when she saw that she was only kidding, she bit her lower lip and thrust the rose beneath her nose breathing deep.

"T-h-haat's all folks!" She looked up in surprise. She'd forgotten all about Paul. "The end of the show. I gotta go." He was bowing deep, standing near the door. "I just wanted to wish you . . ." He gulped. "I mean I wanted you to know we missed you, especially Mr. Fellini. He refuses to let Sally dance in your place. Insists you'll be back in time."

Kristina's smile was too wide, her voice too gay. "Thank you for coming, Paul, and for the rose. It's beautiful." She ducked her head and took a deep breath, her nose buried in its petals. She watched him stumble from the room with a mixture of pity, and she wasn't sure what. Ever since Jill had pointed out Paul's affection for her, she had felt the burden of it. She wished he wouldn't like her so much. He was . . . he was Paul . . . Paul, the boy she'd known all her life. How could she ever get excited about him?

Jill watched him leave. Her eyes held that quiet look of a wild thing, poised, watchful.

"Gosh, I didn't mean to hurt his feelings." Kristina blurted.

"It wasn't all your fault. I hardly made things easy for him with all my whistling and . . . who did you say he was?" Jill's eyes snapped now full of bright specks, "and how did you meet him?"

"David? Oh, well come on over and . . ." Kristina patted the bed beside her. "I met him . . ." The two of them sat talking and giggling for the largest part of an hour. Finally Jill looked at her watch.

"Good grief! I told Ma I'd get dinner. I gotta go. Take it easy, Kristy." She waved as she dashed out the door.

Kristina leaned back smiling to herself. A friend like Jill . . . she was lucky. Absently she picked up Paul's rose to smell and noted that it had begun to wilt. She leaned over, pushed the buzzer and waited. That was odd. Usually a nurse came right away. She rang it again. Kristina became aware of a commotion in the hall and strained forward listening. Still no one came. She put the rose on the stand. She'd get her own water. She slid out of bed gingerly wincing as she moved. Things weren't as bad as they'd been. As a matter of fact, she had this crazy sensation of itching all over, but from the inside. Maybe that was a sign she was healing.

Slipping her feet into her gold scuffs, Kristina collected the rose and glass and headed for the hall. She moved slowly. All the nurses were gathered around the main station laughing and talking in such excitement that Kristina couldn't help but be curious. She made her way toward them.

"You should have heard it." The nurse's voice was full of triumph. "I thought I was going to faint, but there he was smiling, saying, 'My name is Morey. My name is Morey.' Those were his very words. He's going to make it back all the way. I know it! I can feel it. He'll even walk!"

Kristina stared at the nurses. Their faces were bright in some unknown triumph. Some of them were crying openly.

"What happened?" she asked the nurse standing next to her. She didn't respond. Kristina reached out and touched her.

"What?" The nurse jumped at her touch.

"I'm sorry. I didn't mean to interrupt. I just needed some water and when no one . . . what happened?"

"Oh, I was so excited I didn't hear your bell. Here, I'll get it."

"That's all right. I don't mind." Again Kristina echoed her question, "What happened?"

"It's fantastic! A miracle. Hey," she turned to the other nurses. "Can I take Kristina to see Morey?"

"Sure, he'd love it."

The young nurse steered Kristina down the hall toward a large ward. She stopped in front of a bed. The small black figure was but a dusty smudge in its whiteness. She stood very still looking down at the little boy as if he'd been risen from the dead. "This is Morey." She said it with such reverence, as if she were introducing Kristina to God himself. She looked from the boy to Kristina whose puzzled expression was etched in the wrinkles across her brow.

"Of course, you don't know the story of Morey. He's been here for six months. He was in an auto accident. Killed his sister and injured both parents but not seriously. The doctors gave him no chance. When they saw him that night, they put what they could back together, but they didn't even know how to measure the damage. They had no idea if he was deaf, blind, the amount of brain damage. The predictions were he wouldn't last the night. When he did, they extended it day by day, still not giving him much hope. Finally they agreed that if he lived, he'd never be able to function. We were feeding him intravenously; his bowels didn't function or any of his other natural muscle movements. We did everything for him even to breathing there for the first six weeks. He finally got so he could breathe on his own, but that was it. He didn't focus his eyes or show any evidence of hearing. His parents gave up hope after the first couple of months. I don't blame them. They used to come to the hospital and spend hours just watching for a sign, any sign of change or progress. Finally they stopped coming and the doctors stopped testing."

"What happened?" Kristina stared at the tiny figure. He seemed so small, so . . .

"Well, that was it. We didn't know what to do, but we were bound and determined so we put his crib right next to the nurse's station, the busiest place in the hospital. Every time we went by, we'd stop and talk to him. We'd ask questions. We'd sing songs or wave or shake the crib. This went on day after day without a sign that he heard or saw anything. Finally one day Ruth noticed that his eyes had begun to follow us, and then he looked frightened when Jenny dropped one of the bedpans. When we had to move him out of the hall, we put him in front of a television set and kept it on and all of us made a special effort to go in and talk to him whenever we could."

"It was about a month ago that he smiled, actually smiled at us and seemed to be able to recognize us individually. We told him our names and the names of our children and pets and today . . . " She paused looking at the little boy with such love that it filled Kristina and she felt the excitement. "To-day, he spoke. Betsy was telling him all about her little boy and he smiled and said, 'My name is Morey.'" The young nurse was so overcome by it that her tears rolled unchecked down her cheeks. "Isn't it wonderful?"

She lay very still. The sounds of the hospital had quieted to a low hum. Night muted voices and bells, even emergencies. The story of Morey had swept throughout the hospital with such joy that even the janitors and aides who usually went about their chores with sullen disinterest were caught up in the miracle. Kristina lay, eyes wide, staring at the stucco ceiling, but seeing the tiny figure of a single black boy, hair

123

curled tightly about his ears. The object of a miracle. Of so much love and determination from strangers, from people who did not even know him, but who loved him and fought for him so long and so hard never giving up hope. Always believing. Kristina began to cry quietly. Why? Why couldn't she be like that? Where was her hope and determination? Why had she bought the moonstone?

19

Kristina walked along the beach picking her way through the piles of brown slick-looking seaweed stepping on the bulbous ends trying to pop them. Her efforts scattered the flies that settled over the debris in shifting waves of gray movement. The smell of it twitched at her nose. Not an unpleasant odor, but a briny sea smell that was now and then laced with the heavy stench of the decaying carcass of a dead sand shark or bird that the gulls had yet to pick clean. Kristina bent, selected a long whip with a full round end and began spinning it over her head like a Mexican cowboy twirling his bola. She became caught up in the motion spinning herself around and around. Finally she let it go and watched with satisfaction as it sailed out over the breaking waves back into the sea.

She walked a few feet farther through the soft, cool sand and then picked her way down to the hard-packed surface and started to jog. Throwing her head back, Kristina breathed deep, filling her lungs. As she ran all her tension dropped away and she felt free, as free as the gulls that circled above her. Running had become routine for her ever since she had returned from the hospital. What a relief it had been to escape the clanging bells, the antiseptic odor punctuated by the constant paging voice echoing up and down the halls.

She lengthened her steps into long, smooth strides. Her rhythm was natural, easy, her breathing deep. She lifted her face to the sun as her muscles expanded and contracted. There was no room for thought when Kristina ran.

At the edge of the sand cliffs she paused to rest perching lightly on a large piece of driftwood. The gulls that had been flying high above her swooped lower and lower hoping for a morsel. Kristina marveled at how they dipped and rolled. Everything about them seemed so effortless, a ballet of motion so tuned to their world of wind and sea. Kristina never ceased to be awed by their perfection. This was what life was intended to be . . . perfect unity.

The scene was shattered suddenly when a gull screamed, tucked its wings, and dove straight toward Kristina. Instinctively she flung her arm up to ward him off, but the last minute he changed direction and dove behind her. Her heart thumping wildly, she rolled off the log. Another screech was added to the din. An injured gull dragging one wing was running crablike across the sand. The diving gull caught it broadside and sent it reeling and screeching. It was back on its feet instantly trying to make its way to the cover of the log where Kristina had been sitting.

She was hypnotized by it all. The diving gull repeated his attack over and over. As she watched she noticed the injured bird no longer ran erratically but seemed to have developed a pattern of defense. He lay very still as the gull dove moving only in the last minute to avoid the outthrust claws, and then as the bird climbed to repeat its attack, the injured bird scurried closer to the protection of the driftwood.

It would not survive, of course. There would be other predators, cats, and now that it could no longer fly . . . pity replaced Kristina's curiosity and then anger. A peculiar anger for it was directed at the crippled gull, the intruder to the peace she had been feeling. How dare he spoil the perfectness of it all. She got up to leave turning her back on the gull. She picked her way down to the wet sand and turned toward home.

The screech of attack and cries of anguish stopped her after a few short steps. The anger she had been feeling grew stronger, but now it was against the attacker. Kristina's cries were added to the din as she changed directions running after the attacking gull. She stopped. The bird in the sand lay quivering near the log. She stooped and scooped it up. The bird was so exhausted that only silent cries, cries that she felt rather than heard came from its beak that opened and closed in distress.

The bird's heart pounded rapidly through the soft feathers on his breast. Stroking it gently, she tried to quiet it. His glassy, black eyes blinked in fear. The attacking gull continued its circling, swooping at them screeching angrily. Annoyed, Kristina stooped, gathered up some pebbles and threw them driving off the antagonizer.

She continued down the beach cooing and stroking the bird that she held close to her breast. To her delight it quieted beneath her touch. As she neared home, she looked up the cliff to the house. The sun had dropped low creating long shadows with darkening edges. The last rays lingered on the slick surfaces of the upper windows reflecting a coppery-gold salute.

There were two figures out on the upper deck, one bending over the other. Her father must have brought Anna out to enjoy the sunset. The peaceful contentment Kristina had enjoyed disappeared. In its place came the despair that had become a part of her.

But her father never complained. He was so patient, so loving . . . once again the sight of him reaching out to that lovely dark woman, laughing with pleasure, alive. Kristina tried to swallow her bitterness, the anger she felt for her father, for herself, for . . . she held the crippled bird close to her cheek and stroked his smooth head. "I'm sorry," she whispered. "I'm so sorry."

She made her way through the dusky, quiet rooms seeking her father's advice. What was she to do with the gull? She opened the door and stepped out onto the deck expecting to find the two of them. Instead she was greeted by the sight of her mother's chair pushed up against the railing near the spiral stairway that lead steeply to the rocky garden below. Its emptiness confused her. For a moment staring at it her breath caught with excitement. Hidden within all her despair was the wild hope that one day she'd come home and find her mother walking, laughing, living. She looked around. The shadows had deepened. The only sound that of the surf.

Kristina's skin raised in small prickly bumps and her excitement changed to foreboding. She stood rooted to the spot and then, unwilling, was being propelled by some unseen force toward the empty chair that had become her mother's home. She reached out hesitantly to touch it but could not force herself. Her hand dropped. She paused listening. Had she heard something? Kristina moved around the chair and looked out over the edge of the deck.

Her scream rose slowly like a bubble trapped deep beneath the surface of the sea. The limp form of her mother hung halfway down the stairs caught up in the ironwork of the railing. Kristina dropped the injured bird ignoring his squawking and fluttering, pulled and jerked at the chair trying to get it out of the way, all the time screaming for her father. Finally, half falling, half climbing, she reached her mother. She could not control the sobs. She clutched and pulled at her. "Annya . . . Annya. Oh, Mother." Her father's shadow loomed over her at the top of the stairs. "Help me, Daddy. Help me."

128

"Oh my God . . ." Then he was next to her helping, lifting, carrying.

Kristina lay in the darkness eyes wide staring. No! She closed them. She would not let the thought come into her mind again. Instead the doctor's face floated before her. His concern, assurance. "She's okay. No broken bones. No additional injuries that I can see. A little rest." But for all her determination, there it was again, hidden in the doctor's question, "How did it happen?"

Of course she believed him. She pushed away that niggling doubt. Shaking her head, she tried to free herself of the silhouettes, the shadowed figures, one leaning over the other, but it was still etched too vividly. It remained even after he explained the ringing telephone that had called him inside, away from Anna leaving her, not where the chair had been found, but close to the door. Kristina groaned.

No. She rolled over burying her face in her pillow. He wouldn't. Again his laughter and smiling face drifted before her. His hand reaching out. *He couldn't have!* Kristina spoke the words aloud sitting up among the tangle of her bedclothes. Her thoughts horrified her almost as much as his insinuations had that day on the cliff. What kind of person am I, she thought, who could think such a thing of my own father?

She saw him again with Anna. His tenderness, his thoughtfulness, and dedication. She remembered him helping her with hurt animals and sick birds . . . the sea gull! Kristina was out of bed picking her way through the darkened house toward the deck. She opened the door and stepped out into the damp night air.

There was no moon to cut the night. Kristina called softly, cooing, "Where are you?" Her eyes, accustomed to the darkness, searched the inky corners of the deck. She moved quietly calling softly. The sudden movement almost beneath her feet startled her. "Oh, there you are." The bird tried to escape, but she trapped it against the wall.

"You must be hungry and thirsty. Poor thing." She cuddled the gull close to her breast. Kristina was in the kitchen breaking up bread crumbs when her father came in. He moved from the darkened hallway into the lighted kitchen. Dark circles showed halfway down his cheeks. Her breath caught. She had never seen such despair.

"What are you doing?" He saw the bird.

"I think his wing is broken, Daddy. I was bringing him to you tonight when I . . . I don't know what to do with him."

He looked at the bird lying helplessly on the counter near Kristina. "Wring its neck and put it out of its misery!" His words were loud and raspy. He turned and disappeared into the hall.

Kristina, mouth agape, stared after him.

"He didn't mean that." Martha entered the kitchen tying her robe about her. "I saw the light and wondered if you might be needing me."

"Did you see him?" Kristina's voice was a tiny whisper. "He looked so . . ."

"He needs you, missy."

She paused for a moment staring into the darkness that had swallowed her father. "Here," she thrust the bird into Martha's hands and disappeared after him.

She found him in his office standing in the darkness looking out through the wall of glass. The ocean was obscured by the thick, moonless night. Even the sound was muffled by the heavy air. She paused in the doorway hesitant, confused. If only . . . her thoughts were stilled by the sound, a muffled, strangled . . . he was crying. Shock washed through her. Her father was crying. Kristina flinched from the pain.

"Daddy?" He did not turn. She stumbled through the

darkness her own tears blinding her, washing away her doubt. "Oh, Daddy."

They clung together weeping. It was a long while before their tears subsided, but still they held each other close. The clock ticked hollowly punctuating their despair. Finally her father released her, turned on the small low light over his drafting table and shuffled through one of his drawers. He found a box of tissue and passed several to Kristina and took some for himself. The room echoed with their sounds and then Martha was at the door.

"I thought the both of you could be standing a hot cup of tea with a wee bit of bracer and lot of sugar for you, missy."

They sat quietly for a while both sipping, thinking, and suddenly it was very clear. Kristina gasped with the thought. "It's Anna!"

Her father lifted his eyes. "It's got to be." She rushed on. "That time on the cliff and now again. I didn't. You didn't. It's got to be Anna. But why?" Kristina knew before the echo of her words was lost in the silent shadows of the room. "It's my fault," she whispered through trembling lips swallowing at the guilt she felt.

"No, kitten." His voice was very tired. "It's nobody's fault. Come on," he lifted her gently from the chair. "We have a bird to tend to."

Kristina returned to her room. Exhausted, she climbed into bed and fell into a deep troubled sleep. Everything was black except for the soft white light shining in the distance on a strange object Kristina couldn't quite make out. She was struggling toward it, but the air was so heavy that she had to swim through it to pull herself forward. What was it? She struggled closer. The brilliant blooms of the ice plant were accented by soft maidenhair fern and tall jack-in-the-pulpit nodding. But that couldn't be. The ice plant grew in full sun in dry, sandy soil. The fern grew under the trees in damp, boggy areas. She continued to struggle closer to see what the plants shaded, protected. There at last, she looked down into a coffin, half-buried, the lid partially closed. Inside lay her mother, the woman she knew. Smiling, eyes sparkling. Her lips were moving. She beckoned her to come closer. Kristina kneeled and leaned forward.

"The moonstone, Kristina," she whispered. "Give me the moonstone."

Kristina reached out slowly, the moonstone nestled in her hand. Anna reached for it. Kristina strained forward, stretching, stretching. Her fingers touched the cold, icy coffin. She recoiled as if she had been burned.

"I can't," she cried. "I can't!" Before her eyes the figure changed into the unresponsive, distant-eyed person that sat in the chair staring out over the sea.

"No! No!" Her screams ripped through her. She was struggling, struggling. Kristina awoke soaked in perspiration, the moonstone clutched tightly to her breast.

20

Kristina and Jill sat on the beach. Silently they watched the waves as they built into great troughs, crested and broke into a turbulent spray rolling up on the beach, then rushing back to sea to do battle with the next wave leaving bubbles of foam to burst slowly on the hissing sand.

"Did you see that old movie on TV last night?" Kristina didn't look at Jill but continued to gaze out over the water.

"You mean the one with Jane Fonda?"

"Yes."

"All but the very beginning. What was it called?"

"They Shoot Horses, Don't They?"

"That's a weird title."

"What did you think of it?"

"It was good. She's a good actress."

"I mean the story. Did you think he should have shot her?"

"No."

"Why not? She wanted to die."

"Maybe she did at that very moment, but then don't we all have those kinds of feelings. God, if all our wishes came true . . . I mean you probably wouldn't be here now. Haven't you been so low at times that you wished you were dead? I'm glad there's no one standing at my shoulder with a gun."

"You wouldn't help someone die? What about Pioto and his potions?"

"That's different. I'm not sure that he ever used it even, and then it would only be for the hopeless cases, the ones who were suffering."

"She was suffering."

"From what?"

"Life, I guess." Kristina shrugged and pulled her knees up closer beneath her chin.

"That's absurd. If life's an affliction, well, I guess, we all suffer from it. Living can be hard work sometimes, but don't you think the rewards are worth the effort? Just to have a friend to love, a family, to be able to sit here and talk, sharing, watching the waves . . . "

"But if you aren't happy . . . "

"Happy? What's happy?"

"I don't know. I suppose, well, I guess, it's something different for everyone."

"Yeah, well how long can it last? Happiness I mean. I will get up feeling great and then I come down and Mom gets on my case about leaving my sneaks in the hall, my books on the stairs, and how come my skirt is so short? Presto, I'm not happy. I'm miserable."

"I'd be happy if my mother would just yell at me about anything. She's so miserable I think she wants to die. Jill . . ." Kristina paused for a long while trying to make up her mind about something and then went on, "You'll think I'm terrible, but sometimes I'm tempted to help her. There's been a couple of times when I think she's tried and maybe . . . I mean if she's so unhappy . . . I know I'd want to die. No way would I want to live half a life. Never to be able to run or dance. I think he was right to shoot her."

"You're wrong, Kristy. That's a cop-out. You gotta fight. You gotta make her fight. You gotta yell and scream at her and shake her into wanting to live."

"But how can I do that when I'm not so sure I'd want to?" Kristina's eyes were narrowed searching her friend's face as if she could find the answer somewhere hidden in the set of her eyes or the tilt of her nose.

Jill reached out and took her hand. "You're no quitter, Kristy. Not you."

21

Kristina could not stop grinning. She brushed her hair quickly and then ran down the stairs and into the kitchen where her father sat with his coffee and morning paper. He had been so withdrawn since the last accident with Anna. So very quiet that she had begun to worry about him. She'd made every effort to cheer him up. Told him all about Jill and their latest discussions. Even talked about her ballet and Paul, how Jill thought Paul had this thing for her, but nothing seemed to help. Surely this would perk him up. David could cheer anyone up and he was coming. Coming to meet Anna.

"Guess what, Daddy." She rushed on not giving him a chance to answer. "David is coming to visit us. To see Anna. He's wonderful. He's so smart, has so much . . . " she hesitated, "feeling. You should see him with Allison and Billy. He never gives up hope. He says . . . "

"You forget, kitten, I've met him."

Kritina blushed. "That's right. He's so . . . "

"Handsome?"

"Daddy!"

He reached out and covered her hand. "I'm teasing. I'm sure he's brilliant, and I'd really like to meet him again. What time is he coming?"

"Four this afternoon. It's the only time he can get away."

"Oh dear. That's bad."

Kristina's smile froze on her lips as she watched him reach into his pocket and take out his appointment book. "Wouldn't you know. Peterson. I can't possibly hang him up."

The warmth Kristina had felt drained away taking with it the excitement. Disappointment and resentment filled her. The "Do not disturb" sign was back between them. Why had she thought they could form a relationship on anything but his terms? Angrily, she reached for a piece of toast and started spooning applesauce thickly over the top. As she licked her fingers where it oozed over the edges, she glanced up into his disapproving face. He didn't say anything. He didn't have to.

"I'm sorry, kitten. It just can't be helped."

She continued licking her fingers noisily almost defying him to say something. When he didn't, she shrugged, "No sweat, Daddy. It's not a professional call anyway. Just a friendly visit."

She gulped her juice and hurriedly wiped her hands on her napkin. "Gotta rush. Bye." She brushed past him, snatched up her books from a nearby chair and was about to leave when his voice stopped her.

"I'm really sorry, Kristina. Tell you what, I'll call . . . "

"Don't bother, Daddy." Her voice was cold, impersonal. "Like I said, it doesn't matter." She turned and was gone.

"What's with you?" Jill lounged against the wall watching Kristina.

"What do you mean?"

"The excitement. What you all excited about?"

"I'm not excited."

"Like fun. I haven't seen so much emotion in you since I slammed the locker door on your finger. What's cookin'?"

"Nothing special." Kristina shrugged. "David's coming over."

"David who?"

"Dr. Feldman." Kristina's voice was filled with impatience.

"Oh. *That* David."

"He's coming over to see Anna."

"You'd never know it."

"What?"

"That he was coming to see your mother."

"Oh, Jill, I'm not interested."

"Sure you're not. He's kind of old isn't he?"

"Not that old."

"But too old for you—"

"I don't see why. He's only twenty-seven."

"I thought you weren't interested?" The bell rang shrilly. Jill pushed herself away from the wall. "Off to Mr. Boyd and our special contemporary literature. Guess what he recommended we read?"

"What?" The two girls moved easily along the hall through the throng of students.

"*Fear of Flying.*"

"You're kidding! What kind of class is this?"

"It's a special English class. Had to have approval from home, so now when I come home I'll just tell Mom it's literature. She had her Lady Chatterly and we have our Isadora."

"Maybe you'd better slip it into the house in a plain brown wrapper. Meet you for lunch, outside? Usual place?"

"Sure. See ya." Jill ran sliding through the door as it was being closed.

Kristina sat impatiently watching the clock. It must have stopped. Finally the bell rang. She was the first one out of the room almost running down the hall. She spun the combination furiously. Missing the first time, she had to slow down to get it right. She threw her books, all but math, into the jumble of sneaks, sweaters, and papers that littered the bottom of the locker, snatched up one of the sweaters and headed for the bus.

"Say hello to David for me. Hey when am I going to meet this guy proper like?" Jill called after her.

"Probably never!" Kristina waved. "I don't trust you!" She ran up the garden path and burst into the house. She didn't call out but hurried toward her room. Martha looked up from the kitchen sink. Kristina paused for a moment. "How is Anna? Did you help her fix her hair and . . . " She didn't wait for an answer but rushed through the hall. Kristina checked her watch and groaned. Fifteen minutes to change her clothes. She took the stairs two at a time, threw her books on to the bed as usual, then bent and snatched them up. She looked around the room, hesitated only a moment before leaning over and shoving them under the bed. She straightened the spread with a couple of quick brushes and turned toward the closet. What should she wear? She pulled her sweater over her head and continued to study the selection before her. She wanted to look . . . well certainly not all dressed up, but . . . Kristina couldn't find the word for it. She wanted to wear some unnoticeable little thing that would make her look spectacular. Casually messy and yet neat. Oh, Jill would say she was crazy, incoherent. Well, Kristina knew how she wanted to look. It was something she'd picked up from Anna. A feeling you had when you looked in the mirror. An altogetherness.

She thumbed through her pants rejecting until she came to a pair of powder blue jeans not unlike the ones she wore. She fingered them for a moment then pulled them from the hanger and held them up. She pulled open the drawers and rummaged. Finally she pulled out a green and blue striped polo shirt with a white collar.

Kristina stood before the mirror alternately brushing and messing her hair. Finally she threw the brush in the drawer and took out a tube of frosted bittersweet lip ice, which she rubbed carelessly over her lips. She studied her reflection critically, dabbed a bit of makeup over an emerging pimple, and checked again. She'd be almost satisfied if it weren't for that little mole on her chin, the funny way her brows arched, and . . . she had to admit that nothing was quite right lately. She didn't know why. The way she looked had never distressed her before. Even her figure was all wrong. She was built like Olga Korbut, that skinny Russian gymnast who looked twelve years old. Who could possibly be turned on by a body like that?

What was happening to her? If she was truly in love, and she had entertained that possibility, why did she feel so disoriented, so critical of what she was? Wasn't love supposed to make you feel beautiful? If only she could talk to Anna. She banged the drawer shut and turned away from her questioning reflection.

Kristina stood before Anna's door. The change that came over her was almost physical. Her excitement disappeared, her eyes shuttered, even her walk changed to a more restrained movement, the fluidity gone. A certain wariness, or was it suspicion, had begun to grow. Ever since the last accident, she had taken to furtively watching her mother. She didn't know exactly what she expected to discover, but she was even more edgy with Anna than before. Kristina's inner turmoil had thickened into a more lumpish, dangerous brew. Along with the guilt, hurt, and bewilderment bubbled a new emotion. Was it anger? Resentment? Distrust?

She took a deep breath, knocked lightly, and entered. "Hi, Anna. I have a surprise for you. This doctor—he's really great—works with the kids at the hospital and does fantastic things for them." Kristina casually picked up the hairbrush that lay nearby and began brushing her mother's hair. "Anyway, he's coming to see you."

"Why?" Anna's voice was dull, uninterested. That familiar tight fist squeezed at Kristina's stomach. Was there anything, anything at all, that would interest this woman? That would put the light back into her eyes or the enthusiasm into her voice? Kristina brushed more rapidly trying to control her frustration.

Anna had always worn her hair very short and curly but since the accident it had become quite long. Even though Kristina brushed it daily, it had become dull. All the coppery fire it had once possessed was washed away. The distant, haunted look, the lost weight and longer hair, this was not her mother. This was a stranger that Kristina struggled to know. As she continued brushing, she searched for the words or deed that would overcome the silence that hung between them like a thick, heavy curtain. The sound of the doorbell echoed releasing her.

She set the brush down hastily calling, "I'll get it, Martha."

Kristina stood before the door hand on the knob, legs crossed. When was she going to outgrow that childish urge to go to the bathroom every time she got excited. The need passed; she took a deep breath, and opened the door.

"Hello, Kristina." She didn't respond. He waited. Then puzzled he looked at his watch. "Am I late? You were expecting me?"

"You came? You really came?"

"Well, yes. I mean this is Wednesday isn't it? We did say Wednesday?"

"Invite him in, Kristina. Don't be making him stand out there in the damp."

"Oh, my gosh. Of course. You're not late. You're right, it's Wednesday. Come in. I'm sorry." She stepped back opening the door wide.

"Hello. You must be that smart, young doctor Kristina has been running on about. I'm Martha." She held out her hand to David who took it in both of his. Kristina could see Martha blushing.

"And you must be that wizard, Martha, who helps solve all Kristina's problems."

Martha's blush deepened. "Oh, go on with you."

"Kristina says you can do anything. Even make her mother laugh."

As she listened to the light exchange between them Kristina began to recover from her speechlessness. He must think her an idiot standing there gawking like a mute. She wiped her sweaty palms on the back of her jeans trying to think of something clever or witty to say.

"What a fantastic house." David paused, looking about him.

"My father designed it. Would you like to see the rest? Come on." She reached out and took his hand. In her eagerness to show the house she had forgotten about her shyness. "Isn't it neat? I love showing it off." She pulled him from room to room pointing out the hidden features, the lighting, the special conveniences of hidden bar, bookshelves, television cabinet. "Each time I take someone through the house, it's like seeing it again for the very first time. It is neat, don't you think? I wish Daddy were here."

They stood in her room looking out over the ocean. Although David was silent, she could feel his appreciation.

"Hello . . . " Kristina started at the echoing call. Her heart skipped. He had come after all.

"Up in my room, Daddy. I was showing David the house." She ran into the hall to meet him. As he reached the top of the stairs she took his hand and held it tight. He smiled. She felt an unfamiliar rush of emotion. "Thank you, Daddy." she whispered and then was dragging him into the room. "You remember David?"

"Of course. How could I forget the doctor who saved my daughter's life? How are you?"

Kristina stepped back and watched the two men shake hands. Her father's long, slim fingers were obscured by David's wide, strong hands. Although Rodney Lowrey rose more than three inches above David Feldman, the doctor's muscular arms and shoulders equalized the height loss with a vibrant strength unusual for a doctor, at least those Kristina had met who were smooth, nonmuscular men with well manicured nails.

"This is quite a house. I suppose you get bored with people telling you that."

"Never." He laughed. "Come on, how about a cup of coffee or tea? Martha's got the kettle on."

Kristina bustled into the kitchen ahead of them. "Don't bother, Martha. I'll fix the tea." She turned, "You did want tea, David?"

"Yes, please." The two men watched her as she set out the cups and poured hot water into the teapot. There was a comfortable silence as she worked.

"Make a cup for Anna too, kitten."

"Kristina's doing a great job with the children."

"Yes? Well I guess that surprises me a bit. I never thought . . . I mean . . . she . . . well with her mother . . ." He stopped struggling for the right words. "She's so new at it and . . . well, it's hard," he finished lamely.

Kristina stopped short, tea bag dangling. The warm feeling drained from her and was replaced with resentment. She studied her father. What right did he have to criticize? What did he expect? It was all well and good that he treated Anna just like he always had, but with Kristina it was different. Things weren't the same. They never would be the same. Anna and she would never dance together again, or surf, or share anything.

David's words cut through her thoughts. "All I know is that beautiful smile and enthusiasm of hers are certainly therapeutic for the children . . . and me."

Kristina began to withdraw, tuning them in and out, listening to their questions and answers as if they were strangers overheard on a bus. She sorted and cataloged the information about David: two older sisters; one younger brother; father, a logger; expected two more years in residency specializing in physical and psychological rehabilitation of the handicapped. She busied herself pouring the hot tea into mugs. "Cream or sugar?" she asked placing the steaming mug in front of David.

"Neither, thanks." He didn't even look up but reached out cupping his hands around the mug seeming to relish its warmth. They were talking about Anna. Kristina might as well have disappeared as far as either of them was concerned. David's interest consumed his entire body tipping him forward like a diver poised at the end of a board. Finally satisfied, he sipped his tea thoughtfully. "I'd like to meet her."

Kristina tagged along unnoticed as they went to Anna's room. Her mother didn't turn when they entered. Rodney went over to her. "Hello, Anna." He leaned down and kissed her on the cheek. "How have you been?" He didn't wait for her response but continued. "You have company." He turned the chair.

Kristina watched her mother smile politely and extend her hand casually to David as her husband continued the introduction. "Dr. David Feldman, a friend of Kristina's." His voice was full of the same pride and warmth it had always contained when he introduced Anna to a colleague or friend.

"Mrs. Lowrey." David took her hand in his and smiled that wide, gracious smile that did funny things to Kristina. "I can certainly see that your daughter comes by her beauty naturally." The words should have sounded corny, but they didn't. "I've been wanting to meet you for some time. Kristina has told me so much about you."

Now that wasn't true. Why did people say things that weren't true? She watched them closely. Anna's eyes brightened the way they used to for Kristina. She felt a painful twinge. Her mother did not pull back from David but left her hand in his.

"I can't say the same about Kristina." Anna actually smiled. "And I can see why. I would want to keep you all to myself too." She didn't look at Kristina but kept her eyes on David's face.

Of course she was joking, but Kristina swelled with indignation. That wasn't true. It was her idea to bring David here. She had hoped that Anna would respond to him like everybody else, and she was—so why didn't Kristina feel happy? She couldn't believe what she was feeling as she watched her mother actually flirt with David, lowering her eyes and patting her hair.

The conversation went on about her, but she didn't hear. She swallowed at her misery. She didn't believe or understand her feelings. Suddenly it was too heavy.

"I'm going to take Jonathan down to the beach," she interrupted. Her father smiled and waved, but Anna and David didn't even look up. She turned and fled them all.

22

Jonathan, that was what she had christened the gull, had become a member of the family. She and her father had trimmed his shattered wing close to his body. Although he did not regain perfect balance he learned to handle his loss quite well. He became comfortable with his home on the deck and it wasn't long before he accepted them all, even Martha who scolded him often for his nuisance. He ate from their hands, perched on Anna's and Kristina's shoulder, and talked to them in soft, throaty chirps.

At first her pity had been overwhelming. Whenever she saw a gull soaring or diving into the sea, she swallowed her tears her heart aching for his loss. And then she was frightened for him. How would he survive? But Jonathan fared very well. He hardly lacked for food with all the scraps they provided him. All in all he seemed quite content. Only once had Kristina seen him cry out against his loss. Two gulls had perched on the deck railing. The three of them talked in their peculiar way and Jonathan became very excited. When the birds flew away, he spread his one good wing running along the deck trying to launch himself. As he tumbled, Kristina heard a long, wailing screech. She ran over and picked him up and held him close trying to comfort him.

When she opened the door to the deck, Jonathan fluttered toward her squawking his greeting. She stooped extending her arm for him. He hopped up immediately bobbing his head and talking to her in his low throaty tones. As she ran her finger over his head, he closed his eyes his voice growing softer and deeper. Kristina tilted her head and brushed her cheek with his soft feathers.

"You want to go to the beach?" It was almost as if he understood for he became excited fluttering his good wing and bobbing his head while opening and closing his beak. He looked like a miniature rooster about to crow.

The beach had become a routine for them. At first she had been worried that he'd run away, but it turned out quite the opposite. If he got to scratching along the debris line looking for morsels and she moved too far away, he'd let out a scolding squawk and chase her down. He'd indeed become one of the family.

Kristina sat huddled on her rock her knees drawn close to her chest. She watched Jonathan as he scratched contentedly. So engrossed was she with her own thoughts that she didn't hear David come up and was startled when she looked up to see him standing quite close to her. He didn't say anything at first, just stood there studying her, and then said softly, "What's the matter, Kristina?"

She ducked her head pulling her knees up even tighter to her chest. "Nothing," she mumbled. God what would he think of her if she told him. Even she was horrified at herself. He would think she was . . .

He stood there a moment longer then moved past her down to the water's edge and started to jog. "You coming?" he called.

She hesitated for a moment and then was up off her rock extending her cramped legs. She ran a few stiff steps and was halted by Jonathan's scolding. She stopped and waited for the bird, scooped him up, perched him on her shoulder, and then began to run again. Her stiffness had faded and her strides became easy and smooth.

She caught up with him and they moved side by side neither looking at the other. The only sound was that of their feet against the sand and their breathing echoing faintly into the rolling surf.

The two of them jogged effortlessly for a while and then David stepped up the pace forcing her to break into a run to keep up. He lengthened his strides even further into long, smooth running steps that quickly left Kristina behind as he moved out easily outdistancing her. She tried to increase her pace, but her lungs began to burn in protest, her legs to tighten. Even Jonathan protested as he clung to her shoulder. It was no use. She could not catch him. She did not stop but rather returned to the smooth, easy pace that she found comfortable and continued down the beach after David's shrinking figure.

He turned heading back toward her. They met, stopped, perspiration glistening. Both of them were breathing deeply, their chests rising and falling with exertion. Kristina turned starting back toward the house. Without a word he fell into step beside her.

"You father tells me you and your mother were unusually close before the accident, but now, well, now things are different."

It wasn't a question, but she could tell he expected her to answer. She paused, bent, and picked up a pebble. With deliberation she threw it out over the rolling breakers. "I can't talk with her anymore." Her words were flat, matter-of-fact. "She's built a wall between us, shut me out."

"She built the wall?"

"I suppose you're like father; you think it's all my fault." She had stopped and stood facing him her eyes narrowed. She could not hide her resentment.

He reached out and took her hand. "Kristina, it's nobody's fault. There are no simple answers." She could feel the tears beginning to rise and she wanted to turn and run, but he held on to her and continued. "Does she still help you with your ballet?"

"Don't be silly." Kristina jerked her hand away. "She's crippled. How can she help me?" She didn't wait for his answer but turned and started down the beach. He caught up and they walked a ways in silence. She didn't want him to say anymore, to ask her any more questions, but he didn't stop.

"Yes, Anna's crippled, but that doesn't mean you can't share something else besides dancing."

"You don't understand. Dancing is everything."

"They why not let her dance through you?"

"When she can't even walk? Don't you think that would be cruel?"

"You seem to be all caught up on the fact she can't jump or leap about like you."

"I know her!" Kristina's voice rose close to hysteria. "She's like me. Watching somebody else do something she can't . . ." She threw up her hands in frustration at not being able to make him understand. She resumed her walking.

He wouldn't leave it be. "It takes time to get past the crippled part you know. You're not the only one that finds it hard." They walked on silence settling between them. But David wasn't through. "Why didn't you stop running?"

"What?" She looked puzzled.

"Back there. There was no way you were going to catch up with me, yet you kept running. Why?"

"Well, just because I don't run as fast as you doesn't mean I don't like to run."

"It wasn't important that you keep up with me or catch me?"

"At first it was. I really tried. I wanted to, but I couldn't."

"But you didn't stop." It was more of a statement than a question.

"No."

"Why?"

She paused examining his question then shrugged. "It's like I said, I just like to run."

"You don't think there's something about ballet that Anna could still enjoy?"

"When she can't even walk?"

"Kristina," there was impatience in his voice, "her brain isn't crippled."

Puzzled, she stopped and studied him, her brows drawn together. "You don't make sense," she sputtered and turned and ran up the path.

He said good-bye to Anna and her father. Kristina followed him to the door. He stood on the porch. "We'll see you Tuesday?"

She hung on to the door. "Is there any use?" Kristina didn't look into his face but stared down at the floor. "Like you say, I can't get past the crippled part."

He smiled and tilted her chin making her look at him, "Oh you will . . . you will." He leaned over and kissed her on the cheek and then was gone.

23

"You know what I think?" Jill lay back on the grass hands beneath her head. The soft medicinal smell of the eucalyptus trees permeated the air still damp from the morning fog. She breathed deep. "Ahhh, smell that."

Kristina raised her head, sniffing. "What?"

"The eucalyptus. Can't you smell it?"

"Oh, that. Sure. How can you not smell it?"

"You'd think I'd get used to it, but I never do. Every time I smell it, I think of grandfather. He puts a lot of stock in the medicinal power of the eucalyptus."

"You believe that?"

"I don't know. It's probably as good as some of the stuff they dish out today. Grandfather says the only person who can cure you is yourself, and I guess if you think rubbing eucalyptus oil over you or drinking eucalyptus tea will do the job, then who knows, maybe it will."

"You really believe people can actually think themselves better?"

"Or worse. Sure. How else can you explain all the hypochondriacs in the world? If only the sick went to the doctors, Medicaid would probably have a surplus and all the doctors you know wouldn't be driving TR Sevens or Mercedes Benz."

"Not all of them."

"Oh, I forgot. What does *he* drive?"

"A Pinto."

"Yuck! No class. Besides, give him a year or two. He hasn't even started. How was his visit?"

"All right, I guess. Hey, how did you like *Fear of Flying?*"

Jill rolled over. Continuing to chew thoughtfully on a piece of grass, she propped her head on her hand and studied Kristina deliberately until Kristina began to fidget under her scrutiny. To cover her agitation she sat up and hugged her knees rocking gently back and forth. "Well, was it as pornographic as they claim?"

Jill didn't budge. Wouldn't let Kristina run. "You never talk about her. Why?"

Kristina looked away. Avoiding Jill's eyes, she busied herself brushing imaginary grass from her skirt. "I don't know what you mean."

"Bull! Hey, it's me, Jill Hangtree, granddaughter of powerful medicine man who can see right through you."

Kristina pulled her knees tighter, rested her chin on them, and for once didn't avoid Jill's eyes but returned her gaze honestly. The silence grew heavy. Neither girl spoke. Finally in a small, low voice Kristina said, "I can't."

Students milled about them laughing and talking, but the two of them were oblivious. Jill sat up abruptly, reached around to her stack of books, picked one up and tossed it to Kristina. "Here, read it for yourself."

The two of them responded to the ringing bell by gathering up their supplies. Together they walked back toward the building. As they separated, Jill threw up her hand to wave then called after Kristina, "And don't forget the redeeming factor."

Kristina never just sat down to read. She prepared for it like one readied himself for a long journey. First she popped

.. ..arge bowl of popcorn loading it down with butter and salt. Then she found two large firm apples in the refrigerator, washed and quartered them. Finally she poured herself a tall glass of Sprite adding ice cubes and a dash of lemon. Surveying the tray, she nodded in satisfaction, turned out the light, and made her way to her room. She turned back the covers, propped and fluffed the pillows, moved the light a little closer to the edge of the nightstand. Ready at last, she climbed into bed, book in hand, and settled herself with a sigh.

Reading was not one of Kristina's loves. Oh, she could read all right, it just wasn't one of her favorite things. Given a choice, she'd much rather participate physically in life's offerings than intellectually through someone else's experiences. She read her assigned books dutifully but never acquired the library habit.

Wow! Kristina paused in her eating. She read rapidly, slipping her finger under the page ready to turn it long before she had completed the words before her. Of course she knew all about sex. One could hardly go through the public school system these days without being exposed to all the answers. She reached out blindly feeling for the popcorn bowl, grabbed a large handful, and nibbled never taking her eyes from the page in front of her.

"Kristina . . ." The sound of her name had an impatient ring to it, as if it had been repeated several times.

"Huh?" She looked up to the shadowy figure at the foot of her bed.

"Do you realize what time it is? That must be some book."

Too late, Kristina realized and tried to hide it. Embarrassment flushed across her face. "Daddy . . . I didn't hear you."

"I knocked and called three times, but then I guess you were too engrossed." He hesitated for a moment then came around into the circle of light and sat on the edge of her bed.

"Well, tell me, I see you're almost halfway through, what do you think of Isadora?"

She couldn't believe her ears. "Y-you've read this?" She held up the book in disbelief.

"Yes."

"But it's pornography!"

"You're reading it."

"That's different. I mean . . . well I . . . "

"You're young," her father volunteered. The slight smile that had edged the corners of his mouth widened into a grin. "Believe it or not, kitten, curiosity doesn't disappear with age. What do you think of it?"

"Well . . . I . . . " She hesitated searching his face half hidden in the shadows. He waited patiently. "I . . . " She stopped again and then plunged ahead recklessly. "I think it's gross. It all seems so ugly, so vulgar, so . . . "

"Exciting?"

She was surprised. How had he known? It was as if he could feel her heart beating. She giggled. "Well . . . yes, but how can it be both?"

He didn't answer immediately, instead he reached over, took a large handful of popcorn, and began eating. She thought maybe he was going to ignore her question, but after a moment of contemplation he said, "You know, kitten, I'm not sure. After all these years, it's still a mystery. I guess that's what so intriguing about sex, what keeps us interested all our lives. We never *know*."

"I thought it would be so different. I mean love. Isadora, she keeps talking about love and then she does it with two men at the same time. Can that be love?"

"Maybe for her or maybe it's what we used to call having the hots for someone. Physical attraction is no joke. Passion has inspired writers, singers, violence, death. It is nothing to pass over lightly, but to call it love . . . well, I believe that is one of the most abused words of the day. I'm not sure Isadora knows the meaning of love."

Kristina looked down at the book in her hand. She thumbed the pages noisily. "I suppose with the kids being less inhibited today they are willing to try new things like Isadora."

His laughter filled the room echoing off the walls and ceiling. Kristina, surprised and puzzled, stared at him. What had she said? "Kristina, you should read the *Kamasutra* written centuries ago. It makes Isadora look like a nun."

It was too much, her father suggesting she read a book like that. Wait until she told Jill.

"You know, there's nothing wrong with sex, kitten. It is probably the strongest single drive we have. We were created that way in order to perpetuate ourselves." He paused. Kristina watched as he searched carefully for the right words. Finally he went on. "I'm no prude. Of course there's sex without love. Different people practice and enjoy different things but . . ." Again he hesitated, searching. "There's something so special about the sexual act when it is combined with love that makes Isadora's experience pale to mere physical contortions. Without love, well I guess for me sex would be a lot like eggs without salt, or God am I botching this! You'd better talk with your mother." He started to get up from the bed, but Kristina reached out and stopped him.

"Don't go, Daddy, you tell me."

He sat back, reached out, and touched her hair that spread across the pillow. His voice softened and then gruffly, "Kristina, love, sex, caring, it all goes together, especially the caring. It is so personal. There aren't words to describe love. All the words ever written are nothing more than diffused, shadowy descriptions of an emotion so . . ." He spread his hands, "indescribable!"

Kristina started to speak, but he held up his hand. "I know we haven't been close." She bit her lip. "It's difficult to discuss personal feelings about so private a matter, but if there are questions, if I can help, I want you to know I've torn up my 'Do not disturb' sign and thrown it into the fire where it belongs. Something I should have done years ago. Now young lady," he stood, reached for the bowl of popcorn once more and took a large handful, "I know Isadora is fascinating but first things first. You need your rest. Goodnight." He bent and kissed her on the cheek.

Kristina stared where he had stood long after he'd gone. A dreamy look came into her eyes. She reached up, switched off the light, and slid beneath the covers hugging them up around her chin. Her whole body tingled with a strange new sensation. She lay there, eyes wide staring into the darkness. She couldn't stop grinning.

"Jill!" She waved. "Let's eat over here." They sat close together beneath the tree. She handed Jill the book. "I read the whole thing over the weekend."

"And?"

"Wow! Do you think she really did all those things?"

"Isadora?"

"No. Erica Jong. After all writers usually write about personal experience don't they?"

"Maybe she's fantasizing about things she'd like to do."

"Oh." Kristina thought about it for a minute. 'Yeah, I guess so. She's a bit far out though, don't you think?"

"About what?"

"Well, not all of us spend the majority of our waking hours with a mirror between our legs or our fingers in the pit like she says." Kristina giggled at her own vulgarity. "Do you think anybody actually does all that?" She wrinkled her nose. "I mean . . . well . . . sucking you know . . . yuck!"

The whole thought of sex was an unexplored adventure for

Kristina. How could one feel frightened and repelled yet at the same time excited and attracted? She tried on each new idea cautiously rejecting some with revulsion but toying with the possibilities of others.

"Did you find it?" Jill had finished her sandwich and was opening the wax paper around a huge piece of chocolate cake with thick, rich frosting. She scraped the frosting from the paper with her fingers and licked them.

"What?"

"What I told you to look for, the redeeming quality."

"Heavens! There was no redeeming quality about that book."

"I thought so."

"In the zipless..." the word stuck in her throat like a burned piece of toast.

"Hey, Isadora finally rejects that. What I thought was intriguing was her questioning the need she had for having a man. She only felt worthy or whole, so to speak, when she was in love. Don't you think that odd? Why should we have to experience worthiness through the eyes of someone else? Why is it important for us to be loved and needed?"

Kristina paused, banana half-peeled, and studied Jill. "Geeze, I was so shocked by the sex I didn't even think about that."

Jill went on intent on her questoning. "Was that just Isadora's hang-up or do we all have it? Do you suppose boys feel the same way?"

"You mean about sex?"

"No. About needing someone to love them."

Kristina remembered her father sitting on her bed. How he'd made her feel. "I don't think all men are like Isadora's. Maybe they are more casual about sex, but love... some men think it's important." She looked at Jill with new interest. "How do you seduce a man?"

Jill's eyes widened. She hesitated. "Why ask me?"

Kristina smiled. "It's a feeling I have. You know, don't you? You've actually made love to someone?" She was leaning close to Jill waiting expectantly.

Jill eyed Kristina over the wax paper she was licking collecting the last remnants of cake with her tongue. Methodically she folded the paper into precise squares. She tucked it inside the brown lunch sack which she refolded along its creases.

"You know, Kristina, I lost a friend once. It was weird. We were very close. That was before she confided a very personal thing with me. The telling ruined the friendship. My feelings didn't change, but she was so embarrassed about what I knew, that she couldn't look me in the eye. I still wanted to be friends, but she couldn't. I don't want to make that same mistake, because I like you very much."

The two girls exchanged a long searching look, then Kristina looked away. "It's like me and Anna I guess." Her voice was low. Jill had to lean forward to hear her words.

"A little perhaps, but with one big difference." She paused. Kristina looked up waiting for her to go on. "You can't. I won't."

24

Being in love sure wasn't the wonderful thing the songs proclaimed or that Isadora longed for. On the contrary Kristina decided she was in love and it was miserable. For one thing it was cumbersome and tiring carrying another person so totally within you. She didn't like the invasion of her mind. Her thoughts were no longer her own. She decided love was not a blessing at all but an affliction. If she wasn't careful, she could lose her own identity entirely. Kristina resolved to fight it.

She'd ignore David. That would solve the problem. After all if she didn't see him. It didn't work. She stayed away from the hospital and was more miserable than ever. Even Jill noticed.

"Boy are you snappish! Honest, if I didn't know better, I'd say you were on the sour end of an affair."

"What do you mean by a crack like that?"

"See, there you go. Flying off, mad at everyone."

"Oh, go shove it!" Kristina marched off leaving Jill open-mouthed.

She sat brooding in her room. If only she had someone to talk to. Several times she got up and moved toward the door only to come back and flop across the bed. Kristina had never felt like this before. Boy she'd become a real gem. Poor Jill.

And Martha. She lay stretched across the bed staring moodily out the window. The telephone rang. She didn't stir. It
wouldn't be for her. The way she'd been acting, she didn't
have a friend left.

"Missy?" Martha's voice echoed. Kristina crawled off the
bed.

"Hello." The word was close to a snarl.

"Kristina?"

His voice was warm. She could see him smiling. "We've
missed you. You okay? I mean you're not ill?" Her heart was
pounding, her throat dry. She licked her lips. "Are you
there, Kristina?"

"Yes, David. No, I mean I haven't been sick." Her voice
was high and squeaky. "How are you? I've been so busy with
my ballet. We have a recital coming up you know and I've got
to practice, and . . ."

"Well, that's a relief. I was wondering if you'd like to go to
the White Mountains with me this Sunday. I've talked to
Rod and he thinks you'd like it. It's a long drive. We'd have
to start very early, but it's worth it. The bristlecone are really
something."

"What are bristlecones?"

"Trees. The oldest living trees in the world. Once you've
seen them, you'll never forget."

Really it didn't matter what bristlecones were. If he'd ask
her to go up and stare at a stone, she'd have jumped at the
chance. "Yes. I'd like to go." Her words were breathless.

"Fine. Get to bed early."

She didn't believe it. She stared at the phone as if it were a
genie's lamp that had just granted her a wish. Kristina forgot
all about her resolution to stay away from David. Her misery
turned to joy. A whole day. All to herself. She spun about
hugging herself in anticipation.

She came awake with a start her heart beating rapidly.

Had she overslept? She raised up and checked the digital and groaned. Only twenty minutes had passed since she last checked. The night was never going to pass. She lay back and closed her eyes. This time she'd sleep longer.

It was still dark when she kissed her father good-bye and climbed into the car beside David. "I'm sorry to get you up so early," he apologized. "But it's a long way."

It was embarrassing. Kristina wanted to be entertaining and witty. To be sophisticated and mysterious. All she did was sleep. No matter how hard she tried, her eyes would not stay open. Her restless night was only partly to blame for Kristina had this affliction. The car put her to sleep, even on short trips after a long, restful night. She slept more soundly than she had all night. Kristina woke to his gentle shaking.

"Look." They had driven a good distance and were now in the lower foothills of the mountains. The sun's rays angled out from the horizon ahead of them touching lightly on the boughs heavy with hoarfrost. She was silent in her awe. Finally she ventured, "It's beautiful, David. Like . . . " She paused for a long moment. It was no use. There were no words to describe the sparkling, jeweled effect of the sun on the frozen boughs.

"It's like a woman," David volunteered, "or rather how a woman can make you feel."

Kristina caught her breath and looked at him curiously. "I guess a man can make a woman feel that way too."

"Now that I wouldn't know." He laughed heartily and then pointed up ahead. "What do you say, ready for a break?" She followed his pointing to a roadside diner. JOE'S TRUCK STOP. "Like a cup of coffee or something to eat?"

To her surprise she was hungry. Really hungry. Usually she didn't eat much breakfast. Partly due to her lazy sleeping habits but mostly from lack of appetite. That was one thing, she'd heard people in love couldn't eat. Nonsense! Kristina was ravenous. She didn't know what to do. What if he just ordered coffee?

"You hungry?"

"Kinda."

"Well, let's eat breakfast then. Order away young lady."

She looked over the menu. Finally she settled on the Trucker's Special: two eggs, toast, ham with a side of fried potatoes. "Oh," she called after the waitress, "plus a large glass of juice."

David was smiling. "I'm glad you were just *kinda* hungry. Just where are you going to put all that? If you manage to eat all that, you'll look like a boa constrictor that just swallowed a gopher."

"Aren't you hungry?" Suddenly she realized he'd just ordered toast and fruit.

"Breakfast isn't my favorite meal. I usually don't have time. Stay in bed to long."

"Me too. I don't know why I'm so hungry." Her tone was apologetic.

"No problem. I'll probably wished I'd ordered more when I see yours."

Kristina forgot to be shy or worried about what David thought. When she was hungry, there was room in her mind for only one thing—eating. She polished off the last morsel of ham, rubbed her toast across her plate picking up the final traces of yolk, and drained her glass. As she wiped her napkin across her mouth, she looked up and caught David sipping his coffee studying her.

"I was wrong. No gopher bulge at all." Kristina blushed. "But it does amaze me. Must still be growing or else you have two hollow legs."

He was different somehow. At the hospital, even at her home, there was something about David that awed Kristina, but now, in the car driving, just the two of them, she had thought she'd be so tongue-tied she wouldn't be able to utter a word, but it was as if they were old friends. Almost like it was with Jill. He talked about his family. What it was like growing up in the back country of Oregon where he milked cows, helped raise pigs, and teased his sisters with garter snakes and spiders.

Kristina found herself laughing hard and loud over his tales. "I guess growing up on a farm is not so boring after all."

"Boring? What makes you think it would be boring?"

"I don't know. It just seems like there's nothing to do. You live so far away from everything. Even neighbors."

"Well, there's one thing I can assure you, farm kids aren't bored."

It was the knowing way he looked at her that gave Kristina the impression he was alluding to some activity beside riding cows and catching snakes.

She snuggled down curling tight into the seat. She should be absorbing the scenery, after all she'd never been in these mountains before, but she found sneaking glances at David far more satisfying. They had settled into a comfortable silence. David was occupied driving the narrow twisting mountain road. She continued to watch him furtively. How she'd love to run her fingers through his thick blond hair or trace the outline of his jaw with her . . . She ran her tongue over her lips and swallowed smiling to herself.

"What's so amusing?"

"Oh!" The blush flashed crimson. He'd caught her. For a moment she was sure he'd been peeking inside her head.

"N-nothing," she stuttered and turned her face away pretending to concentrate on the scenery.

David gripped the wheel tightly. The spring thaw had created huge potholes in the road. It was a good thing his car was nothing great. She winced as they bottomed out in another huge chuck hole. He swore as he shifted down and they crawled along. Finally, he turned the car into a parking lot. Kristina stretched like a cat waking from a long nap. "Are we there?"

"Not exactly. The best trees are a ways up the mountain. We'll have to hike."

"How far?"

"Not that far. You good for an hour or so?"

"Sure. It'll be great to move around." She climbed out of the car eagerly. "Brrr." Kristina pulled her coat from the back and put it on. She buttoned it and turned up the collar to protect herself against the wind that whistled thinly. Desolation spread out before them, the lonely sound of the wind in the boughs, the barren rock-strewn ground. Dingy patches of snow lay in the shadows of the trees. The blue sky held a rim of clouds over a distant mountain range. Kristina felt a peculiar sense of lightness. David stood silently beside her gazing off into the distance.

"Feel it?"

"What?"

He didn't answer but continued to gaze out over the mountains. She stood silently beside him. Finally he shook himself free of his mood. "Come on." He turned and started up the path.

Kristina followed as he wound his way upward. She found herself gulping the thin air trying to fill her lungs. He stopped often waiting for her. David was breathing deeply too. "We're up over ten thousand feet," he explained. "The air is thin. You have to adjust." They continued to pick their way up through what looked like a dry creek bed.

"This is it." David flung his arms wide. "Methuselah Walk. These are the oldest living trees in the world."

She looked about her. David stood admiring the trees. There must be some mistake. She turned and looked behind him expecting to see a forest of massive, old trees, but instead all she saw was what looked like old dead tree stumps that had been blasted by the wind and sand into smooth pieces of driftwood not too different from the piles that lay tangled on the beaches.

"These are the trees?" She pointed in disbelief. "But they're dead. We came all the way up here to see some dead stumps?"

David reached out and took her hand. "They're not dead. Come here." He led her over to a craggy stump. "Look," and he pointed to a thin strip of bark that ran along the side of the tree. One small branch of scrubby, short, green needles protruded skyward above Kristina's head. "It even has cones. Look. The seeds will grow. Imagine, after all these years— over four thousand years up here on top of the world. Hardly any rain. Only rock for soil. Some of these trees were alive when they were building the pyramids. When Abraham lived. While civilizations were living and dying these trees just kept on growing." The awe in his voice staled the protest that bubbled up in her. Finally she could contain it no longer.

"But it's mostly dead and ugly."

"How can you think they're ugly?" David ran his hand over the smooth, bleached wood of the tree with a touch of reverence. "That's how it survives. In years when there isn't enough rain to sustain it, the tree dies back sacrificing itself until it finds a level of growth it can sustain. We have much to learn. The bristlecone has adapted to its environment better than any living thing. Look, no rain, no soil, and still it lives. Look at that little one there," and he pointed to a scrubby tree less than three feet tall with a trunk several inches around growing in the shadow of a large clump. "Just a baby, right?" He smiled. "Over seven hundred years old."

Kristina's mouth dropped in disbelief. She walked over, bent and touched the sharp, stubby needles. "Seven hundred years?" Her words were full of awe.

The two of them sat quietly on the mountainside looking

out over the valley. The skeletal fingers of a bristlecone
etched themselves against the sky. "Well, what do you think
of the bristlecones?"

She didn't answer right away but searched within herself.
"I don't know. They're different It's hard to think of them as
trees."

They sat in silence with only the thin sound of the wind
whistling about them. The lightness of mood had vanished.
Kristina pulled her coat tighter around her. She felt confused. What was he trying to say?

25

She had tried, tried to dislodge the idea, but it persisted, niggling at her in the strangest ways. One day lying on her bed looking out over the waves, listening to the music from *South Pacific* and dreaming of "Bali Ha'i," it had come again.

Her vision was so vivid. She saw the old Polynesian woman singing while her young daughter danced. True, it wasn't really ballet, but as Kristina lay listening to the words to "Happy Talk" she grew excited. She remembered the loveliness of the lithe young girl dancing with her hands.

Kristina jumped up from the bed, picked up the needle, and started it again. She threw her head back letting the music flow. Closing her eyes, she pictured the children. They could do it. She moved across the room, plopped down on her rug before the mirror, and began dancing "Happy Talk."

Some of it came easily, but there were parts. Kristina struggled listening, trying to remember, to visualize. She closed her eyes and began again. Where she couldn't remember, she improvised. She practiced playing the song again and again. Finally satisfied, she rose and turned off the music. It was good. Eagerness to share her pleasure began to stir within her. It would be hard to wait until next Tuesday for her surpise.

On Monday Kristina stopped in at one of the local florists shops. "What do you do with your old flowers?" she asked the young girl behind the counter and began to explain about the children and her idea.

That night she sat cross-legged on the middle of her bed methodically running the needle and thread through the flowers and greenery. She tied the final knot biting the thread with her teeth and held up the finished lei. It was perfect.

After class Kristina rushed off to the cafeteria to retrieve her box of flowers from the refrigerator. The long box and her stack of books make an awkward bundle. If she didn't hurry, she'd miss the bus. Head down, she rushed through the hall toward the big double doors. As she pushed open the door with her foot, she saw the bus beginning to roll.

"Wait!" She threw up her arm and her books scattered about the steps. "Oh damn!" She stopped and tried to collect them all the time yelling, "Wait! Wait!" But the bus gave one huge belch of exhaust and rolled down the drive.

"Oh hell!" Kristina sat on the curb with a thud. What now? She straightened her books and there on top was the smiling face of Nellie washing the guy right out of her hair. Kristina grew determined. She picked up her books, snatched up the box, and started back up the stairs. She stood helpless before the door. Concentrating, she tried to wedge it open with her toes, but that was useless. Her frustration exploded and she took her foot back to give it a good kick when it opened.

"Ah hah! Temper . . . temper. Allow me." The tall, lanky boy bowed Kristina through with a great flourish.

"Paul! Hey, you missed your bus, too."

"Not me." The words came out in his Donald Duck imitation, and then he stopped, smiled kind of sheepishly at Kristina, and went on in his normal voice. "I've got Dad's car. Need a lift?"

Kristina looked at Paul curiously. It seemed to her there had been a change in him lately. He didn't try so hard. Seemed more content and confident. Although the kids still referred to him as Looney Tunes, she had noticed that he resorted to his imitations and jokes less frequently. He was almost relaxed. Especially with Jill.

"I sure do. I'm on my way to the hospital. Would that be too far out of your way?"

"No sweat. Here, let me help," and he reached out taking the long florist box.

She smiled broadly. "Thanks, Paul. You're a lifesaver." She giggled remembering. "In more ways than one!" He blushed and ran ahead to open the car door for her.

The children could barely suppress their excitement as they sat waiting for the surprise Kristina had promised. "Are you ready?" She stood in front of them holding the long box. They giggled and twitched. Ceremoniously, she removed the lid with a great flourish and lifted out the green and floral leis. The children squealed and clapped their hands as she place a lei around each of their necks. "Now this is to get you in the mood," she explained as the strains of "Bali Ha'i" echoed through the room, "And then I'm going to teach you how to dance."

She continued to place the leis around their necks. Finally she came to Allison. Although the child did not move physically Kristina felt her shrink from her as she held the lei above her. Her eyes dared Kristina to place the flowers over her head. She paused, uncertain, remembering her last dance. The strength of Allison's hate. As she looked from the sullen young girl before her to the eager happy faces of the other children a sudden anger swelled inside her.

It would not happen again. Kristina would not allow Allison to spoil it again. She leaned very close to the child, looked her straight in the eye, and challenging her with her own glare, she placed the lei firmly about the girl's shoulders and turned back to the other children.

"We are going to learn to dance with our hands, our fingers, our hearts. First I want you to watch." Kristina signaled Ruth who lifted the needle and placed it on the record. She settled down in front of the children. The music echoed. "Happy, happy talk." She was dancing. Her fingers moved expertly, gracefully telling the story.

The music stopped. "Okay, your turn." She motioned for the children to imitate. Very slowly she sang the words and demonstrated the finger and hand movements. "Come on now, let's try it." The children held up their hands and began awkwardly to imitate her movements.

"That's it!" She encouraged repeating the simple movments. "You're getting it . . . I think you've got it!" They giggled at her exaggerated accent. "Yes, sir, you've really got it! Now all we have to do is put it to music." As the record started Kristina stood before the first little girl who was about nine. Concentration tightened her eyes to tiny slits as she struggled with the finger dancing. Before Kristina moved on, she smiled, squatted before her, and took her hands into her own, helping her. The girl returned her smile. Kristina moved on.

The surprise in Kristina was quite genuine for she never believed they would be able to do it so well. She glowed with pleasure as she moved down the row of children, smiling, helping, and then Allison was before her, hands in her lap her lip protruding in a sullen pout. The happiness drained from Kristina. It was replaced by the annoyance and anger she had felt earlier. Suddenly she leaned very close to the girl.

"Quitter!" She hissed into Allison's ear. She ignored the surprised look that rippled across the girl's face. "You'll never make it because you're no fighter!" Her words were low, only Allison could hear. "You're soft and weak," she continued.

"I am not!" The girl screamed clawing at Kristina who flinched back out of her way. "I am not!" Allison lunged, trying to hit Kristina. "You . . . you let on that you like us, but I've seen it. You hate the way we are. I hate you!" She lunged again this time falling out of her chair onto the floor.

Ashen, Kristina stood over Allison, as the other children, open-mouthed, stared at the little girl who lay prone beating her fist weakly against the floor. A nudge of realization pushed at the shock that had silenced Kristina. "You talked." It was a whisper. "Allison, you talked!" She stooped and gathered the little girl into her arms and rocked her gently. A surge of joy rushed through Kristina. Tears ran down her cheeks. "You moved, Allison, you pushed yourself out of your chair. You aren't completely paralyzed!"

Allison stopped crying and looked up at Kristina. Her violet eyes were wide pools of wonder. "I did, didn't I?" She trembled. "Will I be able to walk?"

"I don't know, Allison, I don't know. I hope so, and we're sure going to work very hard, aren't we?"

She had to find David to tell him. He would be so happy. She stopped at the nurses' desk. "Have you seen Dr. Feldman?"

"I think he went to the cafeteria."

Kristina rushed down the hall leaping down the stairs two at a time. She swung open the cafeteria door wanting to shout the news. She couldn't wait to fling her arms around David. Her joy caught in her mouth and slowly drained back down her throat leaving a bitter taste.

He didn't see her. She watched as he reached out to the woman. Kristina sucked in her breath in recognition. It was the same woman she had seen with her father that day in the fog and David wore the same admiring look her father had.

He looked up and saw her standing there and waved. She forgot about Allison and why she had sought him out. She wanted to run, but her feet were stuck to the floor. He rose and came over to her.

"Kristina, come I want you to meet somebody." She was being propelled against her will. "This is Dr. Loren. She's a new physiologist here. Pam, this is Kristina Lowrey."

"Oh, I think I've met your father." She smiled as she extended her hand.

Kristina lay in bed thinking about Allison, about Dr. Loren and David. He admired her. She could see that. There was no doubt she was beautiful and smart and . . . Kristina rolled over. She raised up, plumped her pillow and flopped back. She sighed. It was silly for her to love David. For some reason seeing him with Dr. Loren had made her focus on the absurdity of it all. It was all wrong. The timing. But still . . . he was beautiful. The longing tugged at her for a moment and then Allison's face flashed before her. Her smile . . .

Kristina sighed again rubbing the moonstone along her chin absently. Then she was looking at it, holding it up trying to see if it really glowed in the dark. It was a nightly ritual now. The moonstone. Each time she got it out she wondered why? She would never give it to Anna. Or would she? She had come close. Once last week she had almost put it in her drawer by her bed but at the last minute had brought it back. No, she would never give it to Anna for in a weird way it was Kristina's hope. As long as she kept it, she knew that deep within her somewhere hope was not dead, that maybe. . . . She took the stone and placed it carefully back into its tissue wrapping.

26

Kristina looked at him perplexed, not understanding. Mr. Fellini drew his head back in exasperation. "I'll start all over." His words were slow, deliberate as if he were talking to a small child. "It's a benefit. You do know what a benefit is don't you?" He didn't wait for her answer but went on. "The New York Ballet will be here in three weeks. While they are here, they are honoring Mrs. Parksokov, the founder of this school and a longtime patron of the New York Ballet, with a benefit to establish a scholarship fund in her name. For that one show they have requested I recommend a young, talented ballerina to dance the lead in *Romeo and Juliet*. I have recommended you. They just notified me here by cable," he waved the yellow telegram under her nose, "that they've accepted my recommendation, and you are to dance the lead."

It was too much to absorb all at once. Kristina couldn't believe it. Paul was not so slow. "That's beautiful, Kristina!" He had his arms about her lifting her high, his joy for her spread across his face.

She couldn't do it. Fear gripped her. She'd never be ready in time. Three weeks to prepare and it had been so long since she danced Juliet. But Anna would help. The happiness drained from her. How could she ask Anna to help? How could she possibly expect her mother—it would only make her feel her loss all that much more. No, she'd have to do it on her own. Maybe . . . she turned to Paul.

"Would you help me? I need so much practice and . . . oh if only Anna . . ." Her face held a distant, wistful look.

"I'd love to help you. I'll bet your mother will, too. She'll be so excited."

"Oh I can't ask her. That would be cruel."

"But . . ." Paul searched her face. "Are you sure she wouldn't want to help? I mean the two of you always worked together and . . ."

"That's just it. It would be too painful, all those memories." The words caught in her throat. Kristina ducked her head so that he couldn't see her tears. She busied herself unlacing her slippers.

The rest of the students had already left. "I'll expect you to practice hard." Kristina looked up, startled. She'd forgotten about Mr. Fellini. "We'll work out Wednesdays and Fridays after our regular session. You will be good, Kristina!" It was a command. He turned and left marching out in short, precise steps that the students had come to mock.

"He's right, you know." Paul lingered watching her. "You will be good . . . maybe even great."

"You think so, Paul?" She tied the ribbons of her shoes together.

"Of course!" His smile was wide, honest.

"I wish there was a part for you."

"Oh, don't worry. I'll get my break."

All the way home Kristina held the news inside her bringing it into her consciousness to examine, building on it like a sandcastle adding high, lacy turrets and towers, writing headline reviews: *New York Ballet Discovers Kristina Lowrey, Great New Talent,* . . . bowing before standing, cheering audiences, accepting bouquets of roses.

She rushed up the stairs bursting into the house; she ran through the hall straight to Anna's room, and there she stopped. In her mind she burst into the room flinging herself at her mother. "It's happened, Annya! It's happened! I'm going to dance with the New York Ballet! Me! Kristina Lowrey, daughter of the great ballerina Annya!" Her hand dropped from the knob. She'd made a lot of mistakes, done a lot of dumb things like telling her mother she was better off dead, being jealous because Anna smiled, and laughed for David and Martha. She turned slowly away from the door. She would not add selfishness to that list.

In her room she changed into her practice leotard and began going through her records looking for Prokofiev's *Romeo and Juliet*. She put the record on and went to the bar.

No! No! No! That wasn't right. Kristina pushed at her limp, scraggly hair damp with perspiration. She stomped over to the record, and in her agitation, dragged the needle carelessly across it creating a loud screeching noise.

"Hey . . ." Her father put his hands over his ears. "Easy does it. What are you all in a lather about?"

"Oh, Daddy . . ." The news bubbled up from Kristina who had contained it all too long. "You won't believe what happened." She ran over to him throwing her arms around his neck. "They want me . . . lowly little me to dance with the New York Ballet. Do you believe that? Mr. Fellini recommended me out of all his students. It's only three weeks away and it's been ages since I danced Juliet. I'll never be ready."

He hugged her enthusiastically. "That's great, kitten." He held her away, "Have you told your mother yet? She'll be thrilled."

"Oh, Daddy, I want to. I need her help so much, but I can't do that to her. Don't you see how mean that would be with her not being able to dance?"

Rodney Lowrey's hands dropped away from his daughter.

"I think it would be the cruelest thing in the world not to tell her, Kristina. After all she would be so proud of you and glad for you."

"You're wrong." Kristina chewed her lower lip. "It would be one more burden for her to carry and she already has too many. Mr. Fellini will work with me and Paul."

"You're making a mistake, Kristina, cutting her off from your life this way. If she's ever going to adjust, if you are, you both are going to have to accept things for the way they are, not what they used to be."

"No!" The word echoed loudly. "I mean you're wrong, I'm not trying to cut her out of my life. I want to protect her from . . ." She groped for the right word.

"From what? You can't change things by ignoring them. It won't go away. You have to make a beginning."

"You're wrong about this." Kristina's voice was cold. "I know Anna."

"Sometimes when you're so close to someone and you love them so much, you can't see things clearly. I think that is what is happening to you and Anna. You both think you've lost so much but have you?"

"My God, Daddy, she's crippled. That's about the worst thing that can happen to anybody!"

"Is it, kitten?" His voice was soft, his face old and tired.

"One more time, Paul." They stood in Kristina's room before the mirror. Paul, his dark hair touseled, and Kristina, tiny in her black leotard, her hair pulled up into an untidy bun, were soaked with perspiration.

"Oh, come on, Kristina, you've already got it down perfect."

Kristina's face was grim. "No. The grand jeté was not as high as it should have been and the . . ."

"Why do you get so hung up on perfecting each individual move. You should concentrate more on the feeling, the interpretation, the . . ." he shrugged spreading his hands, "the entirety of the whole dance."

She was taken back by his criticism. He sounded just like Anna.

"Look . . ." exasperation rose up and she stood before him, hands on hips, "first things first. I've got to get everything else perfect, then I'll work on the interpretation."

"But don't you see," the music swelled and rolled around them, "you'll never get everything perfect. Let's just dance a few scenes with you concentrating on Juliet, how she feels. Don't stop, no matter how imperfect you think something is."

"Well, I don't . . ."

"Come on," he coaxed. They listened for a moment and then moved together. Their first few steps were controlled, exact, like actors entering the stage. As they became caught up in the music a subtle, delicate change became evident. A metamorphosis changing Paul and Kristina into Romeo and Juliet, lovers caught in the web of their family dispute.

So enchanted were the two dancers that they didn't see Anna in the open door. She sat quietly drinking in the beauty and grace of the story, the music. Gradually the expression on her face changed. Raw hunger and need lighted her eyes. She gripped the arm of her chair tightly. So intense was her reaction that Kristina felt it through her dance the same as she had with Allison. Confused, she faltered, stopped and turned. Seeing her mother with tears running down her cheeks, the savage need so evident, she gasped her hand flying to her mouth.

"Annya . . . " She started toward her mother, but Anna shook her head. A deep, unintelligible sound slid up her throat and she whirled her chair around pushing herself frantically down the hall. Kristina started after her, but Paul stopped her.

"No, Kristina. Give her a moment."

She clung to him. "See, I was right." She wept bitter tears.

Paul would be there any second now. Kristina was so nervous she could hardly swallow. She paced back and forth, checked her watch, went to the bathroom one more time. Along with the excitement was a heavy sadness. Neither her father or Anna would be there to watch. They had argued again, even after Anna's reaction he insisted that Kristina ask her to come to her performance, but Kristina was adamant. He was wrong. He would come only if she asked Anna. . . .

She went down the hall and stood before her mother's door. She would dance perfectly if Anna was there. She would dance just for her. It would be Annya's triumph. After all, she had taught Kristina everything. All those years at the bar together, coaxing, correcting. How stupid Kristina had been to get mad when she tried to suggest different methods. She had been jealous of her mother's ease, her naturalness. Perhaps that was why she chose to be technical, precise, perfect for that was something Anna was not. It was an area where Kristina could be superior. She would tell Anna all these things, apologize for those words that day. Maybe her father . . . the sound of the doorbell interrupted her. It was Paul. She hesitated, then turned away from her mother's door and made her way to the entry.

It was odd how calm she was. She stood in the wings of the curtain waiting for her cue. Her mind was quiet, her thoughts on one person. *For you, Annya. This is for you. All you have taught me, all our dreams. I will create a Juliet that you will be proud of. I dedicate this dance to you.* The music swelled drawing Kristina into its beauty and magic.

Strange. How detached she felt from it all . . . the spotlight, the cheering audience, the bows, faces, flowers.

It was quiet now. The house dark. Kristina lay in her bed staring at the moon's reflection on her ceiling, strains of Tchaikovsky echoing. She threw back the covers and made her way quietly through the house to the kitchen. There she opened the refrigerator and reached in for the roses.

She stood silently looking down at the sleeping figure of her mother. Rays of moonlight slanted across the room touching the edges of Anna's face. Kristina leaned over and laid the flowers gently on the pillow next to the sleeping woman. "These are for you, Annya," she whispered softly. "I love you."

27

Kristina lay on the beach in a secluded cove basking in the warmth of the sun. The unusual hot spell was a welcome change from the normal chilly winds and heavy fog that usually shrouded the beach this time of year. Now that school was out, she spent most of her time with Jill wandering the cliffs above the sea or on the beach. She increased her jogging until she was running almost five miles a day.

She lay on her back an open magazine across her eyes. The warmth of the sun penetrated her skin warming her until a thin film of perspiration oozed bubbling the tanning lotion she'd applied so diligently. She didn't hear him approach. He knelt touching the bottom of her foot ever so lightly. She twitched. He touched it again. Kristina kicked her foot in annoyance then resettled. Again he ran his finger lightly over the callouses she'd acquired from all her running. Kristina grabbed the magazine and in one swinging motion sat up and smacked her unknown irritant.

"Yipe!" He fell back.

"Paul!"

"Don't hit me. I won't do it again, honest." He held up his arm as if to ward off her next blow.

"Oh, Paul, don't be silly. I thought you were a bug."

He looked down at himself and said, "Nope. Not enough

legs." He sat quietly smiling at her. Again she was struck with the difference. What had happened to his twitch? She narrowed her eyes studying him. He didn't look away and for the first time she felt nervous beneath his scrutiny. The hair on his lip was a full mustache now and his hair was longer than she had ever seen it. Not unsightly like some of the boys who had refused to fall back to the shorter hair stye, but soft and curly about the nape of his neck. His sideburns were longer too. What a difference it made. His neck no longer seemed so thin and scrawny. His tan was smooth, even darker than her own. She shaded her eyes against the sun. "What have you been up to?"

He pointed to a surfboard lying in the sand. "I have three weeks before my job starts so I've become a beach bum."

"I didn't know you surfed."

"I didn't until a couple of weeks ago. Just learning. It's not hard. You'd be good at it."

"You think so?"

"Sure. You'd catch on just like that." He snapped his fingers. "All it takes is good balance. The trick is learning to read and catch the waves. You want to try?"

"Sure." She stood up dusting the sand from her legs. "What do I have to do?" She started after Paul who had picked up his board and stood waiting. A squawking stopped her. "Oh, I forgot about Jonathan. I can't just leave him." She bent down and picked up the gull.

"Bring him along."

"You think so?"

"Sure, he can swim."

"Well . . ." she paused considering his suggestion then shook her head. "No, he might get confused or something and swim out where I couldn't get him."

"Let's take him home then."

"You mind?"

"Like I said, I'm just bumming. Come on." He reached out and took her hand.

Kristina couldn't get over the change. The beginnings that she had noticed at school were in full bloom. This Paul was certainly not the Looney Tunes character she had known. She was intrigued.

His strides were so long that she had to hurry to keep pace with him. Kristina's house wasn't far, just around the next point.

"Where did you find the gull? What happened to him?"

"Jonathan? I found him on the beach near the sand cliffs. He had a broken wing and was being hassled by another gull. He lives on our upper deck, the life of leisure I can tell you and doesn't seem the worse for it."

"So he's adopted you for his mother?" Paul looked down at her.

"Seems that way. At least he follows me around a lot. At first I think he really missed not flying, diving for fish, soaring, and all that, but now he seems quite content with his lot. I bring him out here at least once a day so that he can scavenge along the beach. I guess it's not such a bad life."

They turned and started up the path. Kristina opened the door, "Martha?" Her voice echoed hollowly. She stood listening. There was no answer. "Come on." She started through the dining room and out the sliding glass doors to the deck. She saw Anna in her chair and hesitated, then spoke. "Anna?" She walked over to her mother. Paul followed. "Anna, Paul is here." She glanced from her mother to Paul and her heart sank. Paul was like her, he could not hide his pity and for a split second she knew how Anna must feel. Suddenly, Kristina wanted to protect her from it. A flash of anger surged through her, but Paul recovered quickly.

"Hello, Mrs. Lowrey. Isn't this fantastic weather we've been having."

Kristina put Jonathan on her mother's lap. Anna smiled and reached out to touch the bird. "Well, it certainly seems to be agreeing with you; you've changed, Paul."

So she noticed it, too. Impulsively Kristina reached out and brushed a wisp of hair that had blown across her mother's eyes. "Paul's going to teach me how to surf."

"Well, I'm not so sure about the teaching part, but I'm going to let her try anyway." Anna said nothing. The two of them stood awkwardly, both at a loss as to how to continue the conversation.

"Hellooo, and who might this be? Oh, Paul." Martha's face was ruddy, her voice loud and friendly. "I was just about to fix a bit of lunch. Are you hungry?"

"To tell the truth, I think I was born that way." He grinned rather sheepishly, then made a weird face, and he was the Paul she knew, the boy who tried so hard to please, to entertain. It was almost as if Paul had caught himself. He smiled pleasantly. "Can I help?"

"Oh go on with you. What would a great hulk of a boy like you be doing knocking about the kitchen?"

Remembering the dinner Paul and Jill had prepared on the beach, Kristina laughed. "Don't be challenging him too much, Martha," she warned. "He's a genius with a campfire and I kinda suspect he's probably pretty good in the kitchen."

They were back on the path heading toward the beach. Kristina had become quiet. Paul had completely captivated Martha leaving her bright-eyed and flushed. He seemed so relaxed around the older woman, so charming.

"She's nice." He was smiling to himself still flattered by all her attention and obvious affection.

"Martha? You're right. Even though she smokes like a chain and sneaks a nip of Daddy's Scotch now and then, she's marvelous with Anna and takes good care of me and Daddy."

Kristina's praise was without rancor or any of the resentment she had felt when Martha had first moved in. She had become fond of her even though she still irritated her.

They walked together side by side down the narrow path and then out onto the beach. Paul carried his board easily. Neither spoke. The lightness that Martha had created evaporated leaving a heavy feeling between the two young people.

"I'm sorry, Kristina."

"About what?"

"About my reaction with your mother. It's just that she's so changed."

"I know. I can't seem to reach her. It's almost like she is willing herself to die little by little. Actually her condition isn't that bad. The doctors can't understand why she keeps losing weight. I've almost given up hope."

"You can't."

"David, Martha, Daddy, they all live on hope but . . . "

"And you?"

She was quiet considering Paul's question. At last she said, "I don't know. Awhile back I would have said hope was a drug used to keep one anesthetized to the truth, but when I was in the hospital, there was the little boy named Morey."

He listened to her story of the little boy's miraculous recovery. "All because of the nurses' determination, their belief, their hope and love. They did that for a perfect stranger. Something I can't even do for my own mother," her voice broke.

Paul stopped. She wouldn't look at him but continued doggedly down the beach. In two strides he caught up with her and took her by the shoulder, stopping her. "But don't you see, Kristina," he tipped up her chin making her look at him. For a moment she saw nothing but the blue and gray light of his eyes. "It was because they were strangers that they could do that for him. He was not their little boy. What about his parents?"

Kristina thought back. "They stopped coming after a couple of months."

"See. It's natural when the pain is so great, when it means so much."

She looked at him and for the first time since it had happened some of the guilt dropped from Kristina. She took a deep breath and felt light and giddy.

"Hey, are you going to stand here talking all day?" She laughed up at him. "I thought you were going to teach me how to surf!" She grabbed his hand and the two of them ran toward the water.

28

They swam out through the surf playing like a couple of young seals each trying to control the board.

"Here comes one!" Paul sat astride the board paddling it, guiding it, keeping it pointed toward the shore. As the wave began to swell and lift him, he stood up planting his feet, firmly balancing himself with his arms. He leaned forward with the movement, the muscles of his thighs tightening as he guided the board across the curl of the wave avoiding the white crest. He maneuvered the board with ease as Kristina paddled about watching.

Paul rode the wave almost to the shore, flipped the board from beneath him with an easy motion. "Your turn," he called.

She took the board as he directed, sitting astraddle, looking over her shoulder for the proper wave. "Here comes one," she yelled. Kristina felt the excitement as the wave began to swell lifting her.

"Keep it pointed across the swell. Don't let it dive! Look out!" The board dipped throwing her headlong, the wave breaking over her.

She came up sputtering. Paul had retrieved the board and was grinning at her. "Not bad for the first time. You almost got up."

"I did?" She was eager to try again.

Paul yelled directions: "Now. Keep the tip up! Look out!" And again, "Here it comes. Don't get so excited. Watch it . . ." Again, "Don't stand up so soon. Wait until you feel the board moving . . ."

"Oh hell!" Kristina yelled amidst flapping arms and legs as she was tossed into the white water. She came up. The smile was gone. Her face grim.

"Hey, it's tough. Why don't we quit?"

"Never! I'm going to do it if I have to swallow every wave from here to China." She climbed astride the board, watched over her shoulder until she saw the wave begin to swell; then she gritted her teeth, turned the board, and started paddling furiously. Suddenly the timing was right. She stood up pressing her toes into the gritty surface, bent her knees slightly driving the board, guiding it at a slight angle, and she was riding. Her face split into a grin and she let loose a wild yell echoing Paul's cry of triumph. She must have managed a thirty-second ride before the nose of the board was caught by the breaking wave upending her once more.

This time she came up grinning.

"Had enough?"

"Yeah. I didn't realize it was such hard work. You make it look so easy."

"You ought to have seen me the first couple of times. I looked like a thrashing windmill."

They moved out of the water and up the beach to where she had left her towel. Kristina dried herself and then began twisting her hair wringing out the saltwater. "Here," she offered her towel to Paul who stood watching her. He took it and began mopping at his own hair.

"I'm beat." She flung herself on the sand and stretched out. "Ahhh . . ." she sighed wriggling into its warmth. "You'd think you'd stay warm with all that struggling but look at the goose bumps!"

"Nerves. It's not so bad once you get over being scared." He stretched out in the sand next to her.

She propped her head on her elbow and studied him quietly. His eyes were closed against the sun that glistened on the water caught up in the black dampness of his hair. It had begun to dry about the temples highlighting the redness of his sideburns. "You've changed. I guess you know that," she said.

He didn't look at her at first but then rolled over and returned her gaze. The waves seemed to hush, the gulls' cries thinned, and Kristina felt a tightening in her throat. He dropped his eyes from hers and began to draw circles in the sand hooking them together with still other circles.

"Is that good or bad?"

"You know it's good. Before you were so . . . so . . . "

"Impossible. Embarrassing. Stupid . . ." he supplied the words she wouldn't say.

"But how?"

"It's not finished, you know. I'm fighting it all the time. It's so easy to slip into 'What's up doc?' It was such a safe routine."

"I still don't understand how you've managed."

"I guess it was Jill. One day she asked me why I insisted on making a fool of myself when I really wasn't half-bad. It made me face up to me. Here was a rather neat person who thought I wasn't so bad when all along I thought I was hopeless. I'm a dancer. So what's so bad about that? Okay, so I'm not perfect but then who is? This is the routine that I go through every time I feel like a worthless idiot. Perfection is impossible. I'm me and that's what I've been concentrating on. Not what I'm not. It helps. I'm even beginning to like me a little. I guess it's like surfing. Once you get over being scared, the goose bumps don't exactly disappear, but they aren't so devastating. You look at them kinda like old familiar adversaries, and you deal with them. I'm not over being scared, but I'm getting better."

She continued to study him for a moment and then rolled over onto her back placing her arm across her face to shield her eyes from the sun. "The change—it's like a miracle."

He lay back closing his eyes against the glare. "Not really. Miracles come by a snap of the fingers. Accepting what you are can take a hell of a lot of work."

Accepting. The word rolled around inside Kristina's mind. Accepting things the way they were. Accepting people not for the way you want them to be, but for how they are. Accepting yourself. "I guess you're right."

"About what?"

"About accepting. I haven't been able to you know." She raised up and propped her chin on her hand. She studied him deliberately searching his face looking for some clue. "Will I ever be able to accept Anna for what she is?"

He didn't answer right away. Finally, he asked, "And what way is that?"

She shifted her gaze from his face to the soft sand in front of her. She began to draw ridges through it with her fingers. "That's just it. I don't know."

He waited.

"I have this awful feeling that she's trying to kill herself and it's all my fault." Once she had opened the door to her secret thoughts, she couldn't stop the flow. "And the horrible thing is there are times I think maybe we'd all be better off!" She waited for him to say something. When he didn't, she said, "Doesn't that shock you?"

When he spoke, his voice was unchanged. "What makes you think she's trying to kill herself?"

"There've been a couple of accidents, and it's my fault. I never could hide anything from Anna. She knows how I feel, and, Paul, for the first time today when I saw the pity in your eyes, I knew how she felt, but I can't help it. To see her like this, all broken. Daddy says I should just love her and I try, I really try." Kristina rolled over on her side, her back to Paul. She brushed at the tears that rolled down her cheeks. She swallowed and went on in a low voice. "At first I thought being crippled was worse than dying, but now . . . if only I could talk to her."

Paul hesitated. He reached towards her, stopped, and then touched her gently. "It's all we can do, Kristina, to try. You'll find a way." She quieted at his touch.

She lay on her back her arm flung across her eyes. He lay close beside her. Neither of them touching yet each comforted by the other. The sounds of the sea rolling onto the beach, the cry of the gulls, a soothing comfortable silence settled between them as they lay basking in the sun.

"We don't see a lot of people surfing here. I wonder why?"

"The waves aren't as good as on the point."

"Then why did you come here?"

"Oh, there are other things." He rolled his head resting it on the crook of his arm studying her.

"What other things?" Her voice was getting thick as she began to grow drowsy.

"Some very interesting things . . ." She could hardly hear his voice through the warm haze of sleep. It occurred to her that she shouldn't fall asleep, that it was impolite, that Paul . . . but it was too much. The warmth of the sun, the lulling sound of the surf, the tired ache of her muscles all worked against her staying awake.

"Yipe!" Kristina jumped up grabbing her towel and blanket. "Wake up, Paul, the tide's coming in." Both of them scrambled to high ground as the next wave broke sending thin fingers of water invading their sandy resting place.

They settled on a pile of logs watching the waves roll in

190

each one breaking a little higher up the beach. "This is a pretty neat beach you have here."

"I know." Kristina continued to stare out over the water. "Sometimes when I'm out here all alone, I pretend it's mine, that it all belongs to me: the sand, the gulls, even the water. Isn't that silly? This beach has probably been here forever. Indians have camped here and who knows what before the Indians, yet sometimes it's mine. I'm the first to see its treasures, to discover its secrets, and I forbid anyone to step foot on my sand or dream on my logs. It's a silly game." She busied herself folding her towel and blanket.

"Have you ever been inside the caves?"

"What caves?"

"You haven't seen the underwater caves? They're practically under your house right there in the cove."

"How do you get to them?"

"You swim along this narrow tunnel under water. It's kind of scary at first, but once you get inside it's so neat."

"How can you see anything?"

"There's got to be some opening, because there's sunshine in there. It's weird, and beautiful. I haven't explored it very thoroughly. The next time . . . "

"Take me with you." Kristina touched his arm in her eagerness. "I've never seen an underwater cave."

"Well, I don't . . . " Paul studied her through narrowed eyes. "It's kinda scary and sometimes you, you don't have claustrophobia do you? How long can you hold your breath?"

"Come on. I can do it!" Kristina stood and collected her things as if it were all settled.

"I don't . . . "

"Paul!" She stamped her foot impatiently. "If I can learn to surf, I certainly can swim to some old cave." She put on her most determined look.

He shrugged. "Okay, if you say so. Come on." They had to hug the bottom of the cliff on the way back because the beach had disappeared beneath the tide. Paul was quiet. Tiny creases of concern etched his eyes. "Maybe we should wait. I mean when the tide gets really high like this, you have to swim under water a long way."

"Paul . . ." Kristina was so sure.

He spread his hands in defeat. "Okay, okay." They came to the path that led up to her house.

"Let me run my stuff up part way. You wait right here." Her words hung between a command and a question. "I'll be right back." She ran up the path, piled her things on a flat boulder, and turned, almost expecting Paul to have disappeared. She was so relieved to see him standing where she had left him. Kristina waved and raced back down the path. "I'm ready." Her voice was breathless, more from excitement than from her short climb.

They followed the cliff for a short distance and then Paul stopped where the water had cut a wide channel into the rock. She had forded the inlet many times but had never thought of following it beneath the rocky bank.

He studied her for a moment. "You're not scared are you?"

"Scared? Of what?"

"It's a long way under there and it gets dark and presses in on you. If you get nervous in tight places and panic . . . "

"I'm no scaredy-cat." Her words were indignant.

"Okay, now listen. When we first dive into the channel it's pretty wide and you'll feel the tide. It's good now because it's coming in and we'll be going with the current. Grab my ankle and hang on. Don't let go, no matter what. I want you to breathe rapidly to get a good supply of oxygen in your lungs. Like this." He started to demonstrate breathing. "When you feel like you can't hold your breath any longer, pump your stomach and chest like this." She watched his ribs and diaphragm expand and contract. "It moves the air around in your lungs so that it's like taking a new breath. You ready?"

Kristina felt a knot form in her stomach. She nodded, her eyes round. "Okay, breathe." The two of them stood breathing rapidly. "Don't forget to grab my ankle and don't let go. Here we go!" He dived cutting the water thinly. She took one last great gulp and followed. Most of the time when she swam under water, Kristina closed her eyes, but now she was afraid of losing Paul. The light cut through the water surprising her with its clarity. He was moving ahead of her toward the dark, rocky mass. She reached out and grabbed his ankle.

With him half dragging and her swimming they moved into the dark water beneath the ledge. The channel narrowed immediately to the point that she used her free hand and half-pulled, half-swam along the tunnel. The water became so black she could see nothing. Suddenly something slimy rubbed against her face. A scream bubbled from her. In her excitement she almost let go of Paul's ankle.

Kristina kicked furiously and then it began to happen. The fear. It was like she was being held down by a giant hand. The fear swelled to panic and Kristina let go of Paul's ankle and tried to swim up to the surface, but there was nothing but water and rock all around her. She rolled over and tried to turn around. She had to get out! Kristina clawed at the sides and then something grabbed her ankle and was dragging her backwards.

She fought furiously, her lungs aching for air. In her panic she forgot Paul's instructions. It was no use. She opened her mouth. The pain of water rushing into her lungs, the blackness rose within overwhelming her. Kristina felt herself going limp.

There was a great weight on her chest that pressed her

down, down and then nothing and then it was there again. She felt herself being rolled over, and there was a soft warmth covering her mouth forcing air down her throat into her lungs. She began to gag and then she was being pulled upward. Kristina choked as the water ran from her mouth and nose and then the breath came again and again and the choking. She began to cry and gasp. Her lungs burned. She was sitting up leaning over and someone was thumping her on the back. She opened her mouth gulping the air, swallowing. "Paul!"

"It's all right, Kristina. You're all right." He was massaging her back as she continued to gasp. "You panicked; that's all."

"Oh, Paul." She reached out for him clinging to him trying to stop the sobs that rolled up from inside her. She shivered. He rubbed her gently trying to soothe her. His warmth seeped slowly into her and she began to relax. Her crying stopped, her breathing became more normal punctuated only occasionally with a childish gasp. Gradually she became aware of the feel of his hands on her back, with their warmth, their reassurance. Paul's rescuing her was becoming a habit. She continued to cling to him, feeling secure. She looked over his shoulder. The cave was a large grayish cloud of stone walls with thin iciclelike fingers hanging from the ceiling, which was a good fifteen feet above their heads. They were on a wide flat rim of smooth stone that edged a great round pool that swelled and ebbed rhythmically. About six feet above them to one side was another large flat shelf. Beyond the upper shelf she could see two passageways leading from the cave. One became very dark a few steps from the opening. The other was the passageway for the light that illuminated the cave.

Paul pushed her away gently. "Kristina."

She clung to him, not wanting to give up his security. He

continued to rub her back, his chin resting on the top of her head.

"This is all very nice, Kristina, but we've got to get out of here."

"I can't swim."

"You won't have to. We'll follow the light. I think we can get out that way. Do you feel strong enough?" He lifted Kristina gently to her feet.

She swayed for a moment and then stood firm. "I think so."

"Tell you what. I'll go ahead, you follow. If this comes out where I think it does, we're fine. I'll go first and help you through."

"Okay." Kristina let go of his hand watching as he turned and made his way toward the tunnel.

After a few steps, he paused waiting. "You all right? I can help."

"No, I can make it."

"Okay, let's go."

Paul followed the rim around the pool until he found a place where some stones jutted out making a natural ladder. He picked his way up easily and turned, extending his hand to help her. "Want me to help you?"

"Thanks." Kristina climbed the stones lightly and with his help pulled herself up to the ledge beside him. They paused for a moment and then began making their way through the lighted passage that wound upward. Kristina had to scramble to keep up with him. Once she slipped. "Damn it!" Paul started to turn to help. "I'm all right." She scrambled back to her feet.

The passage narrowed quickly so that he was forced to squeeze by some of the rock formations. Kristina followed panting with her efforts. He stopped. "You okay?"

"I think so. How much farther?"

"Not far. But I'm not sure I'll be able to squeeze out or not. It's getting awfully tight." He started to move ahead. "I see the opening. It's just ahead."

"Can you make it through?"

"I think so."

Kristina, head down, was concentrating on her footing. Her lungs ached and her feet were bruised and cut. "Here it is. It's okay. I can make it." His voice drifted back thinly because already his head and shoulders were through the opening. Relief flooded through her with a sigh. She looked up. Paul's feet dangled in front of her. She smiled and then, not able to resist the temptation, reached out and tickled the one nearest her. It jerked in protest. He continued to struggle, inching his way. She reached up and tickled it again. This time he kicked and she had to duck. Kristina giggled.

"Hey, what's going on down there?"

"Nothing, Paul. Nothing."

"You'd better watch it." His voice was edged with laughter. "Maybe I'll just sit here and enjoy the sunshine and leave you down there in that dark, drab dungeon."

She grabbed his foot and started twisting his toes. "You'd better not."

"Okay, okay, I'm going!" He pulled himself through the rest of the way.

She climbed up behind him and stuck her head through the opening. "Ahhh," she flinched. She was eyeball to eyeball to Paul who was lying next to the opening chewing a piece of grass. "Come on out, the sun's great." He lay there smirking at her.

Kristina tried to pull herself up, grunting with her effort. He made no effort to help her. "Come on, Paul, give me a hand." She was breathless from her struggle.

"I don't know. Help someone who would tickle a fella's feet when he was helpless?"

"Paul!"

"Okay." He started to pull himself up, then turning swiftly and catching her by surprise, he kissed her squarely on the mouth. Before she could react he was up looming above her. Grinning, he reached out his hand and pulled her up into the sunshine.

29

Where had the summer gone? Here it was mid-August and nothing much had changed. Kristina pushed her mother along the bluff. Jonathan perched easily on the back of her chair lifting his wing now and then trying to capture the small traces of a breeze that rippled the heavy, humid air. Tiny beads of perspiration formed along her forehead and neck. Kristina paused for a moment, twisted her hair, and flipped it on top her head. If only she had a pin or something. She looked around, patted her shorts pocket, and was about to let go when she noticed the two clips in Anna's hair.

"Could I borrow one of your hair clips, Anna?"

"Sure." Anna reached up and removed one handing it to her.

"Thanks." She pinned her hair securely and then resumed pushing Anna along the path. Kristina studied the back of her mother's head. Strange. These past few weeks she had the oddest feeling. There was a sense of peace about Anna, a quietness that made Kristina nervous.

She stopped at the usual place and turned Anna out to face the sea. The air was thick. What breeze there was, was blowing in from the hot dry hills behind the house. There was no comfort from the cool breeze that usually blew in across the water. Kristina noticed the damp ringlets on the back of Anna's neck. "It's too hot for you here."

"I'm okay." Anna never complained.

"I know. The lower ledge. I'll bet it's still in the shade. We'll go down there."

"Don't bother. It's all right here."

"It's no bother." Kristina maneuvered the chair over the rough shale. "It will be cooler near the water."

Jonathan squawked, lifting his wing. "Oh, you think so, too." She playfully nudged him from his roosting place. Protesting loudly, he fluttered to the ground. "You're getting down right fat and lazy, you know." Kristina pushed Anna back onto the path.

It was cooler. The dampness from seeping ground water kept the ledge dark and moist. The shadows and protection from the hot air moving off the hills was welcome. "Look at the moss, Anna." Kristina picked up a dark, damp stone with a fuzzy, green cap. She laid it in her mother's lap. "And look at that silly little fern." She pointed to the deep shadows among the crevices in the stony cliff where a small, hairy crook of a fern was unfolding itself.

Anna didn't respond. The two of them sat quietly, Kristina on a flat stone near her mother's feet. Jonathan was busily investigating the niches between the stones, looking for insects. The tide had turned creating a small, welcome breeze. The water lapped at the stones about six feet below the ledge where they sat. Kristina, her chin on her knees, her arms coiled around her drawn-up legs, stared moodily out over the water watching the breakers build and then explode over the rock juttings.

Minutes crept by. Kristina grew restless with her inactivity. She uncoiled and stretched lazily and then stared out toward the white, inviting stretches of sand beyond the inlet. She'd love to be jogging, but . . . she looked up at Anna who had begun to nod. She stood up and stretched again. Her mother came awake.

"If it's all right with you, Anna. I think I'll take a short run down the beach. I need to get out the kinks."

"Take your time." Anna paused and then she reached out to her daughter. "Kristy . . ." It was the first time in a long time that her mother had called her that. She stopped. For a moment she thought she recognized the old light in Anna's eyes, but when she looked closer they were shuttered again.

"Yes?"

"Oh, nothing. You have a good run." She hesitated, then leaned down, picked up Jonathan, and started to pick her way over the rocks. Then she retraced her steps and moved Anna's chair back and fastened the safety latch.

"Just in case a big wind comes up," she laughed. "I won't be long. Enjoy your nap, Anna." She moved quickly along the path, jumped across the stones, and picked her way to the sandy strip. Jonathan clung lightly to her shoulder until she got to the sand, then she lifted him off and tossed him into the air. He fluttered to the sand, ran happily to the water's edge, and began scratching.

She moved slowly at first and then lengthened her strides. As she ran she removed the clip from her hair and tossed her head. The wind was lovely, like a soft caress. She opened her mouth, breathed deep, her chest filling easily, her muscles expanding and contracting, her bare feet smacking wetly along the water's edge. She threw her arms wide to embrace the world. Her lips twitched into a smile that lasted only for a moment and then disappeared for she was no longer alone. The ghost of Annya ran beside her reminding her that never again would they run side by side. Never again would her mother fly through the air in a grand jeté or stand beside her at her exercise bar or even walk quietly along the beach at sunset.

All these things that they had shared were gone. Jonathan's loud squawking slowed her strides. "Hurry up you slowpoke!" The bird ran rather lopsidedly fluttering his one good wing, lifting himself half off the ground and then bouncing back. She stopped and began to laugh. She couldn't help it. He looked like those old movies of man's first attempts to fly in some of those crazy old airplanes that rose and fell bouncing along the ground just like Jonathan.

She bent down and scooped up the seagull and continued her jogging to the tune of his soft, throaty scolding. "Okay, okay, I got the message." She slowed down to a walk scuffing her feet through the water as it rolled in. She stopped, looked ahead to the cliffs, and then back toward home where she had left her mother. She hadn't been gone long. Anna would probably still be napping.

Kristina walked back from the water's edge to the soft sand and lowered herself welcoming its hot, smooth surface. She loved the sensation of perspiration running between her shoulder blades and the neat way the sand clung to her damp legs. She stretched out her hands behind her head. The blue sky had a gray heat film. Thin cirrus clouds had begun to form out over the water. Jonathan scratched about content now that Kristina was close by. She was amused by his demands on her and Martha. True, he couldn't fly. *"We're all crippled in some way."* David's words echoed. *"Perfection is your hang-up!"* Jill's disapproving face floated through her mind.

Allison. Kristina smiled. What progress she had made since that day when she had broken through yelling and screaming. "Look, Kristina, I can do more on my braces than some people can do on their legs!" Her face broke into a happy grin as she balanced on the tip of her right brace. "And, maybe, just maybe, they are going to let me try the trapeze. I can do all sorts of things there. Oh, Kristina, I love you."

It was gone. The pity she had carried like a heavy stone

was gone. She thought of Allison and all the children. Now she could look at Billy and hope. She could enjoy the small victories of the other children. Instead of pity, she felt admiration for their courage. She wanted to go back to see the bristlecone pines, for now she was sure she could see their beauty.

She had changed. Like Paul she had worked hard, but . . . Kristina sighed. There was still that same closed feeling with Anna. Why couldn't she be filled with hope for her possibilities? Why did she dwell on the things they would never do, never share? Would she ever be free of the guilt? Would she ever be able to accept Anna for the way she was? Could she throw away the moonstone? The questions floated through her mind, old adversaries she had wrestled many times but had never been able to master. Her eyes became heavy, lulled by the surf and warmth.

It was happening all over. She was back in the sea struggling, the water washing over her, pushing her down, down. Kristina came awake thrashing. It was no dream. The water was all around her rolling her about like a piece of limp seaweed. Confused, she struggled to stand. How? The tide . . . it must be one of those freaky tides. She stood bracing herself against the undertow trying to wipe the sand from her eyes. Thank God it was nothing like the one that had caught her and Anna. Anna!

Fear rolled over her. Surely she was all right on the ledge. The waves were high but not that high! She began to run. Jonathan squawked. She stopped, scooped him up, and headed back down the beach hugging the cliffs to keep above the water. How long had she slept?

It was silly. Of course, Anna was all right. The water was up only a few feet higher than normal, but the fear would not let go. Her lungs ached as she pushed herself to go faster.

She turned the bend and relief flooded through her. Anna was still safe on the ledge. She stopped to catch her breath and then looked again. No! She rubbed her eyes. Kristina stood rooted to the spot watching in horror as the chair moved slowly, closer to the edge. Then the whole thing caught up, as if in slow motion . . . a scene from her dream. Anna tipping forward and falling, falling into the water that lapped at the stone ledge.

"Anna!" The scream split through Kristina's head. She leaped forward flinging Jonathan aside stumbling as she ran over the stones. She didn't hesitate when she came to the inlet that had cut its way deeply through the stones, the one she and Paul had explored, but plunged in, her cries "Anna! Anna!" echoing against the rocky ledge.

She came up searching, calling. The water was even deeper than it had been that day with Paul. Fear spread through her as she searched, and then she saw her mother near the cliff. She swam toward her calling. Just as she reached her, a wave broke over Kristina's head washing Anna from her grasp. She struggled to the surface again. This time she lunged at the floating figure and managed to grab an arm. She pulled her mother close grasping her beneath the chin. With her free arm she started toward the bank. As she struggled a breaker caught the two of them and flung them against the base of the ledge. Kristina gasped and gagged, struggling to hold on, to keep her head and Anna's above water.

"Let me go, Kristy." The words echoed off the rocks, off the waves. "Let me go." Anna pleaded.

She stopped struggling, confusion washing over her. "I belong out there." It was Annya's voice, strange but re-membered. Another wave broke over them and Kristina struggled. It would be so easy to let go. So easy . . . she saw her father's tired, lined face. He was so young. He'd forget.

It was building within her now. All those months of silence, of frustration, of love and embarrassment, of guilt.

"No!" Her scream echoed loud and long. "No!" She tightened her grip just as the breaker hit and they were washed under. Down, down. Which way was up? Confused and panicked, Kristina tried to surface, but it had become dark and she lost her bearings. Anna was struggling against her, struggling to get free. The resistance she felt stiffened her determination. They were being washing swiftly along the underground stream. Realization of where they were, gave her a new confidence. The current was even swifter than when she and Paul had swam it. They could make it if only Anna . . . Kristina clenched her teeth and then mentally she was screaming to her mother.

Help me! I'll never let go. Help me! Anna's struggling ceased and for a moment she was limp. Then, in place of the resistance she had been fighting, Kristina felt a lightness. Anna was helping by propelling herself forward against the walls with her hands much as she had done with Paul. That little help, plus the speed of the water rushing through the tunnel propelled the two figures forward.

With a huge gush they were expelled into the cave. Kristina gasped the sweet air gulping in great swallows filling her aching lungs. She shook her head trying to clear her eyes as she clutched her mother. The entire floor of the cave was flooded up to the rock ledge that aproned the tunnel leading upward. A shaft of sunlight split the darkness.

Exhaustion struck at Kristina with a heavy hand. How would she ever get Anna up on that ledge? Her feet hung like leaden weights pulling at her. She tried to kick but nothing happened. They couldn't make it—after all her struggles. She closed her eyes still clinging to her mother. It was strange. Although numb from her effort a warm sense of peace flooded through her. An acceptance that had evaded her all these months.

The water in the cave surged carrying the two figures upward washing them toward the lighted tunnel. Just as swifly as it had raised, the water receded depositing them gently on the ledge.

Kristina couldn't believe it. It was almost as if some unseen hand had assisted them. The two of them lay unmoving, their raspy breathing echoing against the walls. Relief swept through her. With it came her tears. She wept quietly holding her mother close. As the moments passed and her strength began to return, another emotion grew replacing the relief. Slowly it bubbled and churned until she was so filled with it that she could contain it no longer. She sat up jerking Anna to a sitting position. Her anger came erupting uncontrolled like a spray of molten lava.

"What in the hell do you think you're doing? How dare you be so thoughtless and . . . cruel!"

Anna's eyes opened wide in surprise. Her mouth dropped.

Kristina continued. "How can you be so selfish after . . ."

Her mother's eyes narrowed and her mouth snapped shut. "I was just doing everyone a favor."

"What do you mean by that?"

"You don't think I know how you feel? Can't see the revulsion in your eyes every time you look at me or touch me? And the pity . . . God save me from the pity!"

The breath rushed from Kristina as if she'd been hit in the stomach. She gasped and fought for control. The two women glared at one another their anger echoing through the cave.

"Okay." Kristina's voice was low and controlled. "So I haven't been able to accept this. I've been trying . . . "

"How? By shutting me out of everything we ever shared or cared about. I don't want your doctors, or medicine men, or your goddamned roses!"

"Well!" Kristina pulled away from her mother. "Maybe I have done everything wrong, but *I've* been trying! What have you done to help me? You're supposed to be so wise and loving. Forget about me. How could you do this to Daddy? Have you looked at him lately? He needs you! I need you!"

The flushed, defiant look on Anna's face vanished. Her eyes filled with tears and her lips began to tremble. "You do?" Her mother looked so helpless, forlorn. Kristina swallowed, but she would not let go of her anger.

"It isn't easy you know. Living takes guts and we'll all have to help each other."

Tears were spilling down both their faces. Anna's fingers covered her trembling lips. Her eyes searched Kristina's.

"Oh, Kristy." She held out her arms. They clung to one another rocking back and forth.

"I'm sorry, Annya. Oh, I've missed you and needed you so." She pushed her mother away to look at her. It was then that she saw it hanging about her neck. Not the stone that she had bought, but Pioto's moonstone. Hot anger flashed through her. How dare he! How could he? She reached out to grab it, to yank it from Anna's throat, but stopped. What was the legend Jill had told her about the smoky stone? It promised a safe journey from one world to the next.

"It's true, Annya." Her voice was full of wonder. She fingered the stone almost reverently. "The promise is true. It has brought you back. Oh, Annya, it has brought us both back." Once more they clung together.

"Anna? Kristina? Anna?" The thin echoing slid down the lighted shaft. Kristina broke into a wide grin letting the happiness inside her spill out.

"It's Daddy. We're going to be okay." She jumped up. "Down here, Daddy." She started to clamber up through the tunnel, then paused, turned back, and looked at her mother. "We're okay." Her voice was low and wondering and then it rose to a shout. "We're okay."